D0041264

FINDING LOVE AGAIN

A Finding Love Romance

FINDING LOVE AGAIN

A Finding Love Romance

●

Shelley Galloway

AVALON BOOKS
NEW YORK

© Copyright 2006 by Shelley Galloway
All rights reserved.
All the characters in this book are fictitious,
and any resemblance to actual persons,
living or dead, is purely coincidental.
Published by Thomas Bouregy & Co., Inc.
160 Madison Avenue, New York, NY 10016

Library of Congress Cataloging-in-Publication Data

Galloway, Shelley.
     Finding love again / Shelley Galloway.
         p. cm.
     ISBN 0-8034-9755-5 (acid-free paper)
     1. Ohio—Fiction. 2. Domestic fiction. I. Title.

     PS3607.A42F555 2006
     813'.6—dc22

                                        2005028538

PRINTED IN THE UNITED STATES OF AMERICA
ON ACID-FREE PAPER
BY HADDON CRAFTSMEN, BLOOMSBURG, PENNSYLVANIA

To Barbara Galloway, who's a great
artist, a great mother, and a great friend.

To Erin, who's allowed me to create a
whole town and write stories about the
people who live there.

And to Tom, who loves me . . . even though
I'm always behind on the laundry.

Prologue

Denise couldn't believe he was breaking up with her. "But we're engaged," she protested. "We've made plans. You can't just walk away."

Chad Alexander smoothed back a portion of his thick hair and smiled at her with his head tilted just like it was in those coffee commercials he was so famous for. "It's happening, babe. Deal with it."

His complete lack of sympathy for her feelings was stunning. "But I don't understand."

"I got a new job. A real gig. A five show run on *The Sands of Time*. This is the big time, Denise. I've got no time for girlfriends."

Fiancée. She'd been his fiancée.

As Denise watched Chad stride through the double doors back into the brilliant sunshine, she almost

1

stomped her foot. How could she have thought she'd loved him? Had she really been that dumb?

With a swoosh, the doors slid shut. All traces of Chad, his smile, and his silky hair were gone forever.

And Denise most definitely knew the answer to her question. *Yes.*

Yes, she had been that dumb.

With a sigh, she sat down at one of the chairs of the coffee shop where she worked and gazed out the back window.

California. Warm weather. Palm trees. Sandy white beaches.

She'd been so excited when she'd left her small hometown of Payton, Ohio to move to California. How had all those good things turned out so bad?

All her life she'd been Denise Reece, middle child, the one who looked nothing like Kevin, Cameron, Joanne, or Jeremy. The quiet one. The one with blonde hair and gray eyes. Not as bright as Joanne. Not quite as popular as Cameron. Not as responsible as Kevin. Not as charming as Jeremy.

Denise had been so sick of it. When she was little, when she'd spent way too many car trips getting stuffed into the back seat in between too many kids, she'd dreamed about being an only child.

Not because she didn't love her siblings. She did.

But sometimes—actually all the time—she'd felt lost in the shuffle.

As soon as she finished high school, and after one

year of community college, she set out on her own, following every cliché and leaving for California.

For a while, things had been great. She'd gone to the beach, took a few business classes, and worked in a coffee shop.

She'd met Chad Alexander, up-and-coming actor, and she'd been instantly charmed, though he'd often made fun of her middle-America roots and old-fashioned values.

But she'd been sure she could change him, or at least help him understand her more completely.

Until today. Now he'd left her for a soap opera . . . and on the same day she'd received an amazing piece of news from her mom.

Great Aunt Flora had just passed away. Aunt Flora, who'd only visited them on major holidays and never seemed to learn all their names. Flora, who'd been a real fan of real estate and owned a lot of property throughout southern Ohio—even an old run-down theater in Payton which she had willed to Denise. The shock of it had overridden the sense of loss she'd had for the passing of the remarkable woman.

With a small chuckle, Denise glanced at the letter her mother had enclosed with her own note. *"I saw you in a school play in fourth grade, Denise,"* Flora had written in a spidery hand. *"You were wonderful. And now you're in California, no doubt making your mark there. That is why I'm bequeathing to you my treasured theater. I'd like you to refurbish it so Payton can have a theater once again. Perhaps you could even star in the first production! That would make me smile from up in heaven."*

Denise shook her head in dismay. Somehow Great Aunt Flora had gotten everything mixed up. She hadn't been in a fourth grade play. That had been her sister, Joanne.

And she wasn't trying to act in California, she was trying to figure out what to do with her life.

But now it seemed that Flora, along with a fair bit of coaxing from her mom, had set things in motion.

"Take three months and set things in motion, Denise. And, after you've given it your all, if you decide you don't want to run a community theater . . . donate it to the city."

Give it her all. Three months. Donate it to the city.

"Oh, and don't mind Sally."

Sally?

Who in the world was Sally? Her aunt had really been off her rocker. Folding the paper back neatly, Denise stared at the door where Chad had made his exit and knew her future had been decided.

It was time to go do what she'd been afraid to do; it was time to go home to Payton, Ohio, take over her theater, heal the wounds from Chad, and figure out how she fit into her crazy, meddlesome family.

Denise didn't know whether to laugh or cry.

Chapter One

"The moment I heard that Flora left you this old theater I practically shouted with joy," Daphne Reece told her daughter as they carefully walked across the wooden oak planks that made up the dilapidated stage of the run-down theater. "I knew inheriting this old place would finally bring you home."

Denise tried to smile, tried to feel excitement, but truthfully, she was having a hard time even pretending to be happy about being back in Ohio. Even though it had only been six weeks, she already felt smothered by her family and overwhelmed by the changes that had happened with her siblings.

All were now married, exceedingly happy, and completely confused as to why she wasn't thrilled to be around them all, twenty-four hours a day, seven days a week.

Actually, she was happy to see them. She just didn't want to try and fit in with them all over again. Sighing deeply, she said, "Mom, you do realize that Flora got it wrong, right? That I never was in a school play?"

Daphne Reece shook her head. "Yes, you were."

"No, Mom. That was Joanne in the fourth grade play. She was Lucy in *You're a Good Man, Charlie Brown.*"

"No, you had a part in that play too. I'm sure of it."

"My class helped paint the scenery."

Her mother smiled. "Well, there you go." As she ran a hand over the faded yellow walls, she said, "We all know you have a flair for drama. Just recalling how well you did on the debate team gives me chills."

"Mom, that was Kevin who did so well in debate."

"Are you sure?"

"I'm positive. Kevin gave speeches. Joanne did too. And Jeremy was the outgoing one, Cameron was the popular one. Joanne was homecoming queen, Kevin graduated top of his class."

"I'm well aware of who did what, dear," her mother cut in. "I may have forgotten some details, but I know my children."

Denise knew she should have been a little more tactful. "Sorry. It's just that I never was the one who stood out all those years ago. And Flora only saw us on Christmas and Easter. I think she got confused. I shouldn't have been given this old run-down theater."

Her mom took a breath, like she was all geared up to start protesting again.

With a hand to her mother's shoulder, Denise tried one more time. "You need to face it. Aunt Flora got it all wrong. I shouldn't have inherited this place."

Daphne glanced at her daughter, opened her mouth as if to say something, and then shook her head and turned away. Quietly, the two of them walked down the stairs and, by mutual agreement, sat in a pair of dusty theater seats on the front row.

A cloud of dust rose as they disturbed the long-forgotten fabric, encouraging Denise to once again take a good long look at the inside of the theater.

Large for its time, the old building was two stories, made of wood and red brick, and was big enough to seat three hundred people. Intricately carved poles around the perimeter gave one the impression of being part of a merry-go-round. The red and cream colored décor was even now shockingly bold and vivid. The whole thing made Denise think of old Agatha Christie movies . . . there was just something mysterious and spooky about the place.

Daphne Reece sighed, making Denise turn to look at her. Out of all five of Daphne and Jim Reece's children, Denise was the one who looked most like her mother.

More than once, her dad had hugged her and whispered that she was just as beautiful as her mother, that the sight of her took his breath away, because she reminded him of when he was dating Daphne.

Denise took it as a compliment. Daphne Reece was lovely. Sitting next to her in the waning September sun, her mother looked exactly like she always did. Perfect. Her mom was slim, small boned, and possessed a lovely pair of gray eyes.

Just like Denise.

So how did a daughter who looked so much like her mom turn out so different?

With a small frown, her mother finally spoke again. "Denise, honey, I've been thinking. Maybe we've been pushing you too hard."

"Pardon me?"

"Well, during the time you've gotten back, I've paraded you around like a new toy, and barely let you have time to breathe. Your brothers and Joanne have been doing everything they could to help you forget all about living in California and that horrible Chad. Maybe it's time we gave you a little space."

Now she felt guilty. "Mom, I'm sorry. I'm grateful for everything. Really. It's just that—" She paused as she tried to come up with the right words.

But her mom had already started talking again. "This area is safe and is just a stone's throw from downtown. And, whether you want the building or not, it is yours for now. I think you should move in here."

In spite of herself, Denise started to get excited. The idea of regaining a little bit of privacy did sound good. "I could hire someone to do some repair work, and maybe even move in before the end of October."

"I know just the person to do the work too," Daphne added. "Ethan Flynn."

"Ethan Flynn? I've never heard of him."

"You wouldn't. He just moved here a year or two ago. He owns the hardware store."

"But he knows how to do stuff too?"

"Oh, yes. Joanne's hired him to do some work for some historic houses she's helped to restore and for her own home," she said with a tender smile. "You know, the more I think about it, the more I'm certain that Ethan is your man."

Suspicious, Denise stared at her mom. But Daphne Reece just sat there, looking curiously demure.

"Ethan's place is around the corner from Beagle's Books. As a matter of fact, I think you should go down there right now. Maybe Ethan will have time to stop by this evening," she added with a little clap. "Now, isn't this going to be something? You remodeling your very own theater? Who would have ever thought such a thing?"

Not Denise, that was for sure. "I'll go visit him this afternoon."

"I think that's a fine idea, dear. Tell me how it goes."

And with that, Daphne Reece primly walked away, leaving her daughter to wonder if she'd just been set up.

Chapter Two

Ethan watched the blonde stand in front of his shop for a good three minutes before gripping the door handle. Curious to see what she would do next, he rested his elbows on top of the old wooden counter and watched some more.

With a fierce tug, she pulled hard.

Ethan fought back a smile as she finally read the sign on the door—*PUSH.*

Then she pushed and walked in.

And took his breath away.

She was perfection. Her faded jeans showed off slim legs and blue t-shirt made her eyes look silver.

"Hi," she said.

Had his mouth been open? "Hi," he said right back.

10

Then he realized she was probably in for a hammer or something. "Can I help you?" Yeah, she was just about to take whatever she came for and disappear. Girls like her did not frequent hardware stores on a daily basis.

She tilted her head. "Yes, as a matter of fact. I'm looking for Ethan Flynn."

He couldn't resist smiling. "Then you're in luck," he replied, all thoughts of hammers and hardware fading away as surprise and curiosity won out. "That would be me."

Her eyes fixed on him a little more carefully. "Oh," she said, as if she wasn't sure what to say next.

"What may I help you with?"

Instantly, she smiled. It lit up her face and caused him to stand up a little straighter. "You may not want to know," she said as she approached the counter and held out her hand. "My mother sent me to you."

He shook her hand and tried not to grip it too long. "Because?"

"Because I'm about to begin remodeling the old theater in town."

"The one down on Main?"

She grimaced. "Yep. My Aunt Flo left it to me. It needs a lot of work."

"And you are?"

"Oh," she said, as if she just realized she'd been prattling on about nothing. "Sorry. I'm Denise Reece."

He'd heard all about Denise from her parents, had

even spied a picture or two of her, but seeing her in person, talking to her, made him smile. "Denise Reece has a nice ring to it."

"Stop. I've been teased about my name all my life. When I moved to California, I almost took up my middle name, Rose, but that sounded even worse."

Mentally, Ethan tried out 'Rose Reece' and had to agree. "I like Denise."

Her eyes twinkled before turning serious once again. She ran two neatly filed fingernails along his counter before speaking. "Um, do you have a few minutes to spare?"

For her? Oh, yeah. "I do." Gesturing toward a patio set for sale, he said, "Let's go sit down."

When they were finally situated, Denise leaned forward and looked at him earnestly. "My mother said you've done some work for the historical society and a few other groups in town. She thought you might be able to help me fix it up. I want to live on the third floor for a little while."

She paused and met his gaze. "Actually, I think I'm going to need your help with the whole theater. Within the next few days, I need to decide to either donate it to the city, or to renovate and open it again."

As he thought of her parents' home, with its wooded lot, beautifully decorated rooms, and convenient location, he couldn't help but ask, "Why do you want to live there?"

"Because it's away from my parents." She wrinkled

her nose. "I love my parents, but I've been with them now for six weeks. I need some space. And my great aunt willed me that old theater."

"Are you sure you want to live there? It's probably infested. And," he said, just to see what she would do, "People say it's haunted."

"Say again?"

"Haven't you heard? It's all anybody ever talks about."

"Just because it looks old, dark, and scary doesn't mean it's haunted," she replied, but Ethan could practically see the wheels in her head churning. The girl was worried.

"People have stories," he said.

"I haven't heard any."

"You've been in California."

"It's far, but not *that* far. I would have heard something about a ghost. I know it. Or, at least my sister Joanne would have."

"I guess it's all hearsay," he said, regretting his teasing. He didn't know her well enough to kid, and he really was interested in the job she proposed.

Although he was starting to develop a good reputation for remodeling, so far all of his projects were either for residences or small business. Taking on Payton's theater and doing a good job with it would lead him to requests for bigger projects.

He needed this project, and he needed her to hire him to do it. "Thanks for stopping by. I'd be happy to look into remodeling it."

She smiled, capturing his attention once again. "Thanks. Ghost or no ghost, I feel like I was meant to take this project on."

Ethan had to admire her honesty. And he did have to admit that he was humbled that Daphne would have mentioned him to her. It was hard developing people's trust when everyone knew everyone else in Payton. Since he'd only lived there a good two years, and was still living on a shoe-string budget, most people still considered him something of an enigma.

"So, what are your plans for the theater if you do re-open it?"

"Do some repairs. Make it hospitable. My aunt wanted it returned to its former glory." She shrugged.

"What do you want?"

She looked taken aback by his blunt question. "Maybe show plays there again, though I'm not sure how to go about doing that. For right now, just a little peace and quiet. I need to figure out what I'm going to do with my life."

Ethan immediately felt his interest in her dim. In his experience, the only people who took time to 'figure themselves out' were people who had way too much time on their hands.

It made someone like him, who had always known what he wanted but had never had the means to get there, extremely frustrated.

"It would take a lot of money to do the changes you

have in mind, even the renovations in the attic for your living area," he said.

"That's pretty much covered. My aunt bequeathed me the funds to fix up the theater, as long as I follow her directions. I either need to hurry up and restore the old place to its former glory, or let the city take it over."

Still hoping to find some sign that she had her own goals and plans, he played devil's advocate. "So, how does it feel to be at someone's beck and call from the grave?"

Shocked at his words, a fierce indignation replaced the warmth in her voice. Her back stiffened. "Excuse me?"

"What if you wanted to make it a school, or a church, or a huge house . . . what would you do then?"

"But I don't! I just told you that I want to do just what my aunt asked me to." Her eyes narrowed. "What's the problem? If you don't want this job, you just have to say so."

"Sorry. I don't know why I said that." Feeling a little embarrassed, Ethan realized he had no reason to judge her. He'd done plenty of things lately that didn't make a lick of sense, like moving from Cleveland to Payton. Never in his life had he thought he'd be happy some place so . . . quaint. "How about I meet you at the theater in two days? Around four?"

Slowly she answered, "Okay."

"I'll go by there tomorrow and make some drawings.

Then we can examine the plans together and hopefully come to an agreement."

"That sounds good."

Relief flooded over him when he realized they were going to see each other again. "Great," he said as he stood up, trying not to notice how attractive she was and how long her legs looked in those low riding jeans. He'd always favored blondes with a little curl to their hair.

Luckily for him, the door opened.

Unfortunately, it was Rachel, the woman he'd been dating for the last six months.

"Hi, Ethan," she said, as perfectly groomed as usual. "I was near downtown, so I thought I'd surprise you and stop by."

He reminded himself to smile. "Hey, Rachel." Gesturing toward the woman by his side, he said, "Do you know Denise?"

"We were in high school together. Of course I do."

Ethan noticed she didn't look happy about it.

Denise narrowed her eyes slightly, before giving a little wave. "Hi. How nice to see you again."

Because both women looked mulish, Ethan took over the conversation. "Denise here was just talking to me about doing some renovation work for the old theater on Main."

"I inherited it," Denise explained.

"My goodness. Was that why you finally came back to Payton? I mean, you've been gone for practically forever. Three years?"

"Two."

"I guess it just seems like a long time. I mean, we've all moved on since high school."

"I guess we can't all be cheerleaders all our lives," Denise replied.

Rachel's eyes narrowed, making her look mad enough to spit nails. Ethan swallowed hard. Whatever was going on between the two of them didn't look like it was going to end anytime soon. It was time to get them both out. "Well—"

Both women ignored him. Swinging her brown hair over one shoulder, Rachel came closer. "Did you know I'm an interior decorator? I work with Calloway and Wallace in Cincinnati."

The prestigious sounding name didn't mean a thing to Denise, though she didn't want to admit it. All she did know was that Rachel, with her too-perfect hair and know-it-all attitude made her feel like she was fifteen again, full of pettiness and pride.

Their old rivalry over the cheerleading squad came up with a vengeance. And even though Denise hardly knew Ethan Flynn, she couldn't help but be disappointed that he was dating someone like Rachel.

She took a good three steps toward the door. It was time to leave. But Rachel's words stopped her in her tracks.

"And what do you do, Denise?"

She hedged. "I'm kind of in between jobs now."

"But what did you do in California? I mean you did go to college, right?"

Did a year count? "I worked at a coffee shop in California," she admitted, not ashamed but not particularly proud, either. Quickly, she glanced at Ethan, hoping he would curb Rachel's barbs.

But he looked content just to watch Rachel preen. In fact, all he did was raise an eyebrow.

"Oh. Do you hope to serve coffee here in Payton too?" she asked too-sweetly.

Denise's stomach knotted. She'd never liked Rachel. What did Ethan Flynn see in her? She glanced at him again. He was staring at her openly now, as if she was a bug he hoped to squash.

It brought back every feeling of insecurity she'd ever had, tenfold, and it made her eager to give as good as she got. "If I do start serving coffee, you'll be the first to know," she retorted, matching Rachel's saccharine tone. "Thanks for your time, Ethan."

"No problem," he said.

As she exited the store, taking special care to PULL the door, Denise wondered if she'd just made things better for herself . . . or a whole lot more complicated.

Chapter Three

Denise knew she was being unreasonable, but she couldn't help but feel aggravated with Ethan Flynn and that look he had given her. Why had he stayed so quiet while Rachel had delivered her snide comments?

Though an hour had passed since their meeting, Denise was still recalling every minute. She really wished she had come back with a really good retort.

Of course, she also wished things had gone better in California so she could have said that she was engaged to a famous, wonderful man.

She poured herself an extra large glass of cold Diet Coke and had just taken a refreshing sip when her mother called out to her from the living room.

"So, how was your meeting?"

The soda cooled her body, but not her temper.

"Fine," she said, thinking that it hadn't been 'fine' at all. Well, at least not the second half of it.

As if reading her mind, her mother ventured into the kitchen, the heels of her mules clicking with practiced ease. Eyeing her carefully, she said, "Is Ethan going to help you with the refurbishing?"

"I don't know."

Her mother raised an eyebrow. "What's that supposed to mean?"

"It means he's going to look around and then we'll get together in a few days," Denise said, reaching for the very last of her patience.

"Oh. Well, isn't Ethan Flynn so nice?"

"He's okay."

"Okay? I think he's so personable."

"I thought so too, until—"

"And handsome," her mom interrupted. "Didn't you think he was handsome?"

Even though she knew her mother had nothing to do with her troubles, she couldn't help but wish for a little bit of privacy while she processed everything that had just happened. It was times like these, when she and her mother had resorted to their old ways, that she recalled living in California with more than a little fondness. No one had been standing in her kitchen, second-guessing what she'd been doing. No one had been there to judge her actions.

No one had been there at all, really. She'd managed

to get dumped by her boyfriend all by herself. Her shoulders slumped at the memory.

"Hey Mom, Denise," Joanne called as she entered through the back door.

"Hi, honey," their mom called out.

"Hey," Denise said, feeling like things were just about to get worse. Her older sister had a penchant for getting into her business.

"Hey, yourself." She paused, looking at Denise a little more carefully. "You've got that 'eleven' thing going on in between your eyebrows again. What's wrong?"

"Oh, nothing. I just managed to completely embarrass myself in front of Rachel Penderton."

Joanne pursed her lips. "When did you see her?"

"She was visiting Ethan. Mom, you didn't tell me they were involved."

"I guess it just slipped my mind," Daphne answered as she sat down with her own Diet Coke.

"Well, seeing her was a big surprise," Denise said. "Actually, a lot of things were," she added, pushing aside her earlier wish to live by herself. "Something clicked between Ethan and me right away. Next, Ethan said all kinds of crazy stuff about the theater being haunted. Then, just when I was going to question him about that, Rachel came along, and practically pawed at him in front of me. I ended up both sounding and feeling like I had no idea what in the world I was doing."

As his green-eyed glare came to mind again, she sighed. "The meeting was pretty much hideous."

Joanne took a few good fortifying sips of her own. "In Rachel's defense, she's always been perfectly nice to me. And Ethan does seem to like her too. Not that *I've* ever liked her, Denise."

"She's never had a reason to be mean to you. She doesn't blame you for not receiving a cheer award. Plus, I think she thinks I'm after Ethan. She seemed pretty territorial in his shop."

Joanne grimaced. "Ugh."

"Well, my goodness," said Daphne.

All three took another restorative sip of Diet Coke. "I couldn't get out of there fast enough," Denise admitted.

Joanne looked mischievous. "I hope you didn't give her any ammunition. You said that everything in your life is totally great, right? You just happened to break up with your boyfriend, inherit an old theater, and now you're back, ready to live happily ever after?"

Denise tried to fight her smile, but she just couldn't. "Pretty much."

"Well, look on the bright side. At least you won't have to worry all week what everyone else is going to say. Your conversation is going to be replayed all over town within the hour."

Their mom looked shocked. "Joanne!"

"It's true, Mom," Joanne protested. "Rachel Penderton is the worst gossip in Payton."

Given that everyone in their small town had a penchant for getting into everyone else's business, Denise knew that was saying a lot.

"What did Ethan do when Rachel was being so ugly?" Daphne asked.

"Nothing."

Her mother took another sip. "That doesn't sound like the Ethan I know."

"He was in Rachel's clutches, Mom," Joanne said. "He wouldn't have gotten a word in edge-wise."

The picture Joanne painted of Ethan was humorous. Especially since Rachel had attached her hands to his very nice looking bicep with the tenacity of a suckerfish. "He did look slightly uncomfortable," she amended.

"Well, since we're being so honest with each other, I don't know how well the two of them are actually doing," her mom admitted. Lowering her voice, she continued. "Bob, over at the library, said that Ethan doesn't always look too happy to see her." She glanced around, as if she was afraid someone else was listening. "I've always thought she was kind of clingy."

"Why are you whispering?" Joanne asked.

But Denise was far more interested in what her mother had just uttered. "Library? Why would Ethan be there?"

"Checking out a book?" Joanne said innocently.

"Hush. Mom, what's the story with that?"

"Ethan's at the library a lot. He takes courses over at the community college."

This was news to her. "For what?"

"He wants to get a college diploma. He never was able to get one before, what with his parents being on a tight budget and all. I know for a fact that he's been working really hard."

For a fact? Curiosity piqued, Denise asked, "How do you know that?"

Daphne's cheeks reddened. "Well, maybe because your father and I are helping him out a little bit."

"Helping . . . how?"

"We gave him a small loan."

"Why?"

"Not that it's any of your business, but we really like Ethan, and he's had a lot of hard knocks in life. His parents aren't around and don't have the means to help him."

Her mom was right. Their loan wasn't any of Denise's business. But, on the other hand, her mom was sounding entirely too innocent. "I thought you were just telling us how glad you were not to be paying any more college payments."

"Oh, honestly. Your dad and I helped five of you . . . none of you complained about it, either. It's our business if we want to help someone else."

"It is," Joanne admitted.

Just as Denise was nodding her head in agreement, another conversation came to mind. "Now something else makes sense too," she said. "It's been bugging me all afternoon."

Joanne held on to her glass. "What?"

"When Rachel asked what kind of job I'd had, I felt like the two of them were looking down on me. I'd expected as much from Rachel, but Ethan's disregard took me by surprise, especially since I didn't think he'd care about what I've done in my past."

"Now I realize that he was probably thinking I've been wasting my time, not putting all of my opportunities to good use."

Daphne sipped from her glass again. "Ethan has told me that he's never felt like his reality could keep up with his dreams. Maybe that's colored his opinions?"

"Maybe."

"Speaking of dreams and such, have you decided what you're going to do about the theater?"

Just thinking about the building's old gray siding and worn-out interior made her shudder. "I'm going to go ahead and fix it up," she said. "I don't want to deed it to the city."

"Bravo!" Daphne said with a cheer.

Finally smiling, Denise asked, "Do you think the place really is haunted, or was Ethan just giving me a hard time?"

Joanne answered. "There's rumors that it's haunted by a woman whose reputation was ruined in the 1930's. The story goes that a former lover stole from the theater's office and blamed it on the lead actress there. Sally Somebody-or-other. I think she died in a fall from the stage or something else suspicious like that."

The whole story sounded horrible to Denise. But not horrible enough to believe that the girl was haunting the place. "So . . . you think she's hanging out in the theater?"

"No," Joanne said bluntly. "I mean, I've never heard more than a story or two."

"Mom?"

Daphne leaned back in her chair. "When I was young, we used to go there and listen for the spooks, but I never saw anything either. Though, I do recall Aunt Flo whispering about strange happenings occurring there."

A sense of foreboding barreled through her. "Such as?"

"Nothing too big, just lights malfunctioning after they had just been fixed, props moved." She closed her eyes for a moment. "Hmm. Oh! Some people heard strange screams."

"Just that, Denise," Joanne said with a grin.

Denise groaned. "Only *I* would inherit a haunted theater."

Joanne chuckled as she got up to grab a handful of cookies. "It does sound pretty awful. Well, at least you'll have plenty to do there besides worry about ghosts. If I were you, first thing I would do is repair the front steps. They look like they're about to crumble under someone's feet."

"Now that we have everything with the theater figured out, we can focus on Friday's dinner," Daphne said. "Any ideas about the menu?"

Still thinking about crumbling stairs, Denise popped her head up. "What's Friday?"

"Why, it's the last weekend of the month, dear. "Since we're all so busy, your dad and I decided to put a scheduled dinner on everyone's calendars."

The planning was typical of her mom. That caged feeling of yet another family get-together was typical as well.

Denise stifled the unwanted feeling as she, Joanne, and their mom wrote out menu ideas and grocery lists.

Eventually, Joanne left for her own home, and Daphne went to return phone calls.

Denise decided it was a good time to take a long walk. With little fanfare, she stepped along the sidewalks of her hometown, chatting with a few people, enjoying the breezy fall afternoon. Then, with a start, she realized she was standing in front of Flo's theater.

Her theater.

Recalling that she had the key tucked in her wallet, Denise unlocked the front door and went in.

She paused and waited for a reaction. But, after five minutes of silence, she decided to brave the rumors and confront any lingering spirits. After all, she had plenty of things to do, and it all depended on her not messing it all up with silly ideas of haunted mansions.

As she walked inside, decades of dust and mildew

stirred up in wispy clouds. Though the electricity wasn't hooked up, there was enough natural light to search through everything more closely. Sheets lay scattered around, covering a variety of objects and boxes. The intricate columns glowed in the hazy light, making Denise eager to polish them and return them to their former glory.

The maze of offices and closets gave way to the cavernous space of the auditorium, making Denise feel as if she was about to enter a dark cave. She turned and took the back stairs instead.

This decision brought her to a storage room filled with at least a dozen trunks. The old trunks made her feel nostalgic for simpler times. She found herself looking through them all, charmed by the tags on the clothes and the history of each.

Several dresses had old safety pins with notes stuck to them, signifying different costumes.

Then she opened one more trunk and found a photo album, this one from the 1930's. As she flipped through the scrapbook, being charmed by the old-fashioned writing and clothes, she finally started reading the headlines.

They were all about a gal named Sally McGraw. She'd been an actress in the theater from 1929 until 1932. It looked like she'd even known Aunt Flo.

But what was more disturbing were her clippings. They'd gone from flattering reviews to gossip about her finances and her health. Finally, they described her death.

What really took Denise's breath away was an article written by Aunt Flo. In the article, Flo stated that Sally had been swindled by another actor, and her name besmirched and her character degraded unfairly. Flo said that she was sure Sally was innocent of all allegations. *"If I had more time, I would do my best to find the culprit and clear Sally's name. It's unfair that someone so talented should be penalized for things she didn't do."*

If she had more time?

Denise stared hard at the clipping, then made the decision to take the scrapbook home and study it further. It seemed there was something more than just old memories in the theater, and she was going to find out all about it.

Just as she made that promise, she could have sworn a faint breeze drifted through the room, bringing with it the faint scent of talcum powder.

"Hello?"

Nobody answered.

"I think I'm going to leave now," she said to the empty room, still feeling as if someone or something was watching her.

The floorboards creaked.

Carefully gripping the worn album to her chest, she practically ran out of the room. Just as she reached the fourth step on the stairs, the front door opened. "Oh!" she squealed.

Ethan Flynn stepped into the foyer.

"What are you doing here?" she called down, her heart racing.

"I had some time, so I thought I'd look around like I told you I would," he replied, tilting his head up. He gestured to the book she was clutching. "You all right? You look a little pale."

Denise hugged the scrapbook tighter to her chest. "I just thought I'd do a little research."

Ethan rocked back on his heels. "Oh."

She stepped down to meet him and tried to remember just how irritated she'd been with him a few hours ago.

She tried twice as hard not to notice how attractive he was.

But she still did.

Oh, why did he have to be so cute? And why did she have to notice, anyway? "I was just about to leave," she said when she reached the first floor. "I'm uh, going to take this home."

He held up a notebook. "I was just making some sketches. I'll show them to you when we meet again."

"Okay." Denise tried to only think about refurbishing the theater, tried to only care about that, but as usual, she got sidetracked. There was something that drew her to Ethan Flynn.

Maybe it was because his green eyes were so kind looking or maybe because he looked so comfortable in jeans and boots, so confidently masculine in a way that Chad never was. She told herself to look away, to not say another word, but she couldn't help herself. "So I didn't realize you and Rachel Penderton were a couple."

He looked uncomfortable at that. "I don't know if you'd call us an official couple."

"Just . . . together?"

"Just dating," he corrected.

She wouldn't dare delve any deeper. "Have I thanked you for agreeing to help me with the theater?"

He smiled. "Have I thanked you for the opportunity?"

Once again, she felt drawn to him in a way that was altogether confusing. They'd just met.

And because of that, she once again thought about fleeing. "Well, I guess I'll see you in a day or two."

He held up his notebook. "I'll be ready."

As she stepped by him, she caught a whiff of his cologne. "Goodbye," she forced herself to say.

Chapter Four

Friday night dinners at the Reece house were pandemonium. Babies cried, siblings bickered, and with Mr. and Mrs. Reece, five children, accompanying spouses and children, and assorted other invited guests, there were always too many people. The smart ones got a comfortable seat early.

At least, that's what Ethan had figured out as he sat down on one of the couches next to Dinah Reece, Jeremy's wife, and Bryan's mother.

This was the third time he'd been invited to dinner, and already he had found an ally. Dinah was easy to get along with, had more patience than the average person, and was very good at helping Ethan get to the snacks that were often artfully arranged on the coffee table but quickly consumed by Mr. Reece and his buddies.

After grabbing a handful of pretzels, Ethan scooted so that Bryan could crawl on his lap. As the baby fussed with his shirt, he was particularly glad to have something to keep him occupied.

If he sat still too long, he knew he would be tempted to stare at Denise and recall the somewhat shaky meetings they'd shared.

If you could even call them meetings.

Their first one at the hardware store had been uncomfortable, thanks to Rachel's possessiveness. The second at the theater had been strange because Denise had practically run out holding a scrapbook. Their meeting to discuss plans for the theater had been curiously devoid of any conversation. All he'd been able to do was hand her his notes and construction plans. She'd accepted them politely before mentioning a previous engagement.

That was it.

He'd been more than a little surprised to be invited to the family gathering. Not that Mr. and Mrs. Reece wouldn't invited him, but that Denise would okay it. From his observations, she seemed quieter than the other members of her family and more distant. Why was that? Was it because of the break-up her parents said she'd had in California? Because she didn't know what to do with her life?

Or was she just distant around him?

His thoughts were interrupted by Jim Reece approaching with a photocopy of the building's plans.

"So you think it will only take about a month and a couple weeks to make the top floor livable?"

"I think so," Ethan said, giving Bryan back to Dinah before pointing to various points on the paper. "We already have electric, phone, and plumbing lines. All that really needs to be done is bring them up to code and add some built-ins for Denise. Those rooms are small and the staircase is narrow. I wouldn't recommend her attempting to bring up any more large pieces of furniture than absolutely necessary," he added, thinking how hard it was going to be to maneuver anything large up the staircase.

"And the cost? I also examined the balance sheet. The estimate is much less than I expected, Ethan."

"I'm only charging you for the materials and my friend Jeff's labor."

Mr. Reece raised an eyebrow. "But we didn't ask for that. We'd like to pay you for your time."

"I think we're even. I appreciate all the help you're giving me with my tuition. That's enough."

When Jim looked as if he was ready to debate that point a little longer, Dinah leaned over and diffused the situation.

"Jeremy, come see Denise's apartment plans."

Smoothing out the large paper, Ethan showed the three of them his ideas for Denise's apartment as well as some of the work he planned to do on the main floor of the theater.

Jeremy whistled low when Ethan pointed out places

for the built-in bookshelves, desk, and dressers. "It's going to be like some awesome clubhouse. Perfect for Denise."

The image made Ethan laugh. Denise, with her petite build, tailored wardrobe, and innate femininity looked anything but the clubhouse type. "Perfect?" he commented. "I can't imagine Denise ever climbing a tree or roughing it in a clubhouse."

Jeremy nodded. "She did. Denise was always making forts out of old sheets and sitting areas in her closet."

Ethan filed that thought away. Obviously, the girl who always looked so calm, cool, and collected had a whole other side of her that was worth exploring.

Dinah looked to be enjoying the conversation. Nudging Jeremy playfully, she asked, "Did she ever let her little brother in those forts?"

Jeremy didn't look bothered by the reminder of his age. "Nope. Well, Denise did once, when I was crying over something Cameron did to me."

"I once did what?" Denise asked as she approached.

"Let me into one of your famous forts."

Her cheeks bloomed. "I don't know what you're talking about."

"Oh, sure you do, Dee. Remember how Mom always had to go find you if we were missing any towels or blankets?" Jeremy turned to Ethan. "Denise used to love to take all the old sheets for her forts."

"That was a long time ago," Denise said.

Though he would have loved to learn more about her,

Ethan knew she had no desire to dredge up more childish antics. "I was just showing Jeremy and your dad the plans for your apartment and the theater."

Just as her face had shone with embarrassment, it just as quickly paled. "Oh. I think it's going to be great."

Jeremy noticed it too. "What's wrong, Denise?"

"I'm excited about the theater, but I can't stop thinking about something I found out about its past." Turning to Joanne, she added, "It's about Sally."

"Who?" Jeremy asked.

"Sally McGraw. She's a former actress in the theater. She was actually a friend of Aunt Flora's."

"Now people think she's a ghost," Joanne added.

Jeremy grinned. Dinah raised her eyebrows.

Although Ethan's first instinct was to crack a joke, he didn't dare as he noticed more family members quieting. Mrs. Reece sat on the edge of the couch. Joanne and her husband Stratton leaned forward.

"I know you've been to the theater a couple of times now. Have you seen any traces of Sally?" Joanne asked, her eyes wide. "After we talked, I researched the rumors some more. More than one person claimed they heard someone laughing in the attic."

Denise swallowed. She'd been back to the theater twice since she picked up the scrapbook. Both times, she could have sworn she was being watched. But there was no reason to share that. "I haven't seen anything concrete."

"But . . ." her mother said encouragingly.

Denise looked at her family and knew that she was about to let the proverbial cat out of the bag. If she told them she needed help, they would become completely involved, so involved she'd have little hope of privacy or spearheading the project by herself.

Still, she also knew that they were the best people in the world to help her with some sleuthing.

And she also had begun to realize that doing things alone was overrated.

Clearing her throat, she said, "The other day, I was bored and looking through some trunks, and I found a scrapbook, an old one of Aunt Flo's. There were a lot of clippings about one of her best friends, Sally McGraw."

Denise gazed at each family member one by one. "I think she was jilted by a guy and wrongly accused of something, but no one could clear her name."

"We were talking about this the other day with Denise," Joanne continued. "Some guy ruined Sally's reputation and stole a bunch of money from the theater. Rumor has it that Sally was so upset, she wasn't watching what she was doing and fell from the stage."

A chill passed through Denise. "Flo didn't mention any specifics in her journal or her article just that she was upset about it all." Denise turned to each person. "I think Flo knew Sally was really wronged, but didn't know how to fix things."

Kevin, her eldest brother, leaned forward. "So?"

"Well, I feel kind of sorry for her."

"Do you think there's really a ghost?" Ethan asked. "Do you think she really is haunting the place?"

"I don't know. I just feel like if we're repairing the old place and going to try and make a fresh start of it, it would be nice to repair this Sally's reputation too. I feel like it's the least I could do for Aunt Flora."

Her mom gazed at her softly. "What do you want to do?"

Denise looked at her family and felt a warm surge of hope flutter inside of her. For the first time in a very long time, she felt like she was a real part of the family, that she belonged. They believed her, and understood that Aunt Flo's writings were important to her. "I would like to do some research and find out this woman's story."

"What about the theater?"

"Well, I'm no actress, but I do know that people here in Payton like to do things. I want to follow Aunt Flora's lead and turn it into an amateur theater. We could hire someone to run it, and make it into a real centerpiece in the community."

"There's plenty of people in the area who would love to support that," Joanne said.

Stratton nodded. "And plenty of people who would like to have a place to perform."

Mrs. Reece smoothed an already-perfect strand of hair away from her face. "I read Flora's will carefully before I contacted Denise. Aunt Flo wanted something to happen within three months . . . otherwise, it was to be donated to the city."

"So we have three months to get a lot done," Dinah summed up.

From his spot, Ethan could hardly believe the way the conversation had just unfolded. They'd gone from apartment plans to ghost-hunting to amateur theater groups in no time at all.

Glancing at Denise, Ethan felt his heart going out to her. She looked a little pale and very overwhelmed, both by the tasks ahead of her and because of her gregarious family.

Hoping to clarify things, he raised a hand. "Correct me if I'm wrong . . . I mean, my family never did more together than go to church on Sundays, but am I understanding that we now have three months to fix up a theater, seek volunteers to perform in it, find out what happened to this Sally *and* make Denise an apartment?"

The whole group nodded, like he'd just proposed the easiest set of tasks in the world.

But what made it all seem possible, as far as Ethan was concerned, was Denise's sudden relieved smile. It lit up her face and drew his attention like nothing else in the world. "Thanks, everyone."

Ethan jumped as Mr. Reece slapped him on the back. "What do you say, Ethan? Are you ready to be a part of this crazy group?"

As he glanced at the Reece family, at Denise, looking so excited and nervous, he knew he only had one option. If he refused to become more deeply involved, he'd be sitting at home, with only Comet, his Labrador, for company. "Nothing could keep me away."

Chapter Five

Denise spent the next few days thinking about Flo, Sally, her place in the family, and even Ethan Flynn.

For years, she'd always felt out of place among her siblings. And though it had been her choice to move to California, she'd been slightly dismayed by the way her family had been perfectly fine with her decision to leave.

They'd waved her off, wished her good health, and gone on with their own lives. It was evident that they'd also gotten closer while she'd been so far away.

In some ways, she now felt as if her two years in California had been a complete waste of time. Yes, she'd loved living near the beach. She'd loved the people, the weather, and her friends, but she wasn't sure if she'd made any decisions about her future or come any closer to her feelings about her place in her family.

Now, looking back on it, Denise felt she had merely run away from her problems, instead of confronting them head on.

Of course, she also had thought she'd loved Chad. But now that their relationship was over and she'd witnessed her siblings' marriages, Denise decided that maybe—just maybe—they hadn't been in love at all. Why else would the pain be dissipating so quickly, followed by relief and the constant thoughts of someone blond, green-eyed, and even-tempered?

Ethan. In spite of her wounded heart, she'd been attracted to his easy-going nature, his rugged good looks, and his love of her family.

She loved her family too. And, she'd missed them. She was going to have to rebuild her life just like she was rebuilding the theater. Piece by piece . . . all the while, making room for the future.

As Denise stepped over a pile of sheetrock on the second floor of the theater, she glanced at Joanne and Cameron. "Two weeks have passed and everything still seems crazy. You two have been through things like this before. Tell me the truth. What do you think?"

Cameron sat down on an old step stool. "What do you mean when you say we've been through all this? The construction or the entire Reece family involved in a project?"

His heavy statement made her want to sit down too. "Both."

He gave her a sideways glance. "You sure you want the truth?"

His raised eyebrows made her laugh. "Maybe."

"Okay. Rule number one: be prepared for anything."

Joanne chimed in. "Rule number two: be prepared to step to one side when Mom decides to organize your life . . . especially your love life."

Denise knew she could handle that one. She wasn't going to have a love life anytime soon.

Joanne expounded. "Hmm. Every few days—or hours—someone is going to get into an argument, or make you mad."

"Then Dad's going to try and make you feel better—" Cameron interrupted.

"Before Mom organizes everything all over again," Joanne finished.

Denise couldn't help but groan. Their descriptions weren't earth-shattering. In fact, they were all too familiar. Maybe she'd been rash in regretting her move to California?

Cameron was grinning as he continued. "Be ready for all their friends too. Mary Beth's mom was over at our house almost as much as I was when Mary Beth and I were dating."

"I was surrounded too," Joanne added. "Nobody wanted me to face my ex-fiancé alone. When Stratton and I were dating, I was still reeling from my break-up with Payton Chase," Joanne said. "Every time I went to battle with Payton, one of our brothers was with me." She paused. "I still don't know if that was a good or bad thing."

Denise recalled Joanne's phone calls, how she'd been trying to introduce Stratton to the community while everyone in her family had been worried about her jumping into a new relationship. Joanne and Stratton had to practically sneak around to spend time together. "I don't know if I'm going to be ready for any of this," she admitted.

"You won't have a choice," Joanne pointed out. "Overkill is the Reece way."

Denise slumped, feeling left out. While Joanne and Cameron knew what she was about to head into, their descriptions made her feel more than a little wary. After all, their situations had been quite a bit different. She'd been living on her own for several years, only coming back to Payton for holidays and quick visits.

The rest of her siblings had been part of each other's construction projects, treasure hunts, and engagements. Now, more than ever, she felt like she was living on the outside, looking in.

A sudden, fierce urge to run away hit her hard. "Maybe I should just forget about it all and let the town have the building."

"No way. If you don't take this on, the city will ask the historical society to help out, which means I'll have to be in charge of it, and I already have way too many projects on my plate." Hurling a stern look in her direction, Joanne said, "This is your project. It has to be."

Cameron was slightly more diplomatic. "Besides, Dee, this is your theater. What would you do if you didn't have it?"

Well, that was the million dollar question. It was common knowledge that all she'd done in California was work in a coffee shop and go to the beach. And everyone knew that Chad's behavior had hit her hard.

Now Denise was not only trying to find her place in the family, but also trying to find her future, and her true self.

Just one of those would have been a tough job.

All three were feeling pretty overwhelming.

She tackled the most obvious problem first. "I'm ready to help rebuild the theater, but I sure don't know a thing about running one."

"You could learn. After all, you did live near Hollywood."

"Ha, ha. I'm being serious, Cam."

"I know. But, you've always been good at organizing things . . . and you don't need to be the one who runs it, you just need to be able to hire someone who does."

Did she dare admit she had no idea who to hire for that? "I guess."

Joanne patted her on the back. "Everything's going to work out just fine. I'm sure of it. Your apartment is going to be great. It's going to be compact and super organized, just like you. And you'll get to know that

Ethan Flynn." She fanned herself dramatically. "He is so cute."

"Jo, what does that have to do with anything?"

"Everything. I couldn't take my eyes off of Stratton from the moment he came to town."

"That's different. You and Stratton had reasons to be together, and he liked you too. Ethan is already taken. He's dating Rachel Penderton. Remember?"

"Vaguely." Joanne leaned forward and said in a stage whisper, "If you took away the whole Rachel aspect, wouldn't you think Ethan is pretty awesome, Denise?"

Maybe. If she was in the mood to think about another man. Which she wasn't. And besides, Ethan was too desirable for his own good.

He made her think of roses and sweethearts, all the things she'd given up when Chad had shown his true colors. She was afraid if she took the chance and believed in them again, she was going to be even further away from her dreams of independence and self-confidence, which would make coming out of her shell an even harder proposition.

Grasping for straws, she said, "I think Ethan is pretty pushy. He's slipped into our family with the ease of a shoehorn. He's got Mom inviting him over for meals. I'm not sure I trust that."

Cameron said, "Mom and Dad like him a lot. And they should. He's a great guy. I heard he's also doing well with his college courses. You have to admit, Ethan Flynn is a go-getter."

Joanne nodded in agreement. "Plus, his parents live around Cleveland, a good four hours away. If he's not with Rachel, he's usually alone. And we all know what single guys do for themselves . . . fast food." Joanne tilted her lips up in a half smile. "You're not going to fault a guy for liking mom's home cooked meals, are you?"

Now Denise felt petty. "No."

"I think you really need to consider going out with him."

How had theater plans morphed into dating strategies? "Excuse me. We're talking about the theater. And Ethan's practically engaged."

Cameron coughed. "Even I wouldn't have been interested in Rachel. She's got an agenda on her plate, and it's all about finding a husband. Trust me, Ethan's not serious about her."

"They are so not 'almost engaged.' They're just dating. In my book, that means he's available. And, I saw the way he was looking at you at Mom and Dad's the other night. He's interested."

"I don't even want to think about another man in my life. My last relationship was enough to make me consider life in a convent."

"Not all men are like Chad," Joanne retorted. "Take Stratton."

"Your husband's great. And you are too, Cameron. I just don't think the time is right."

"Ethan has a great future," Joanne added. "In fact, I heard his hardware st—"

"Stop! I really don't want to talk about Ethan Flynn right now."

"Oops, does this mean I better leave?"

Denise just about fell off her stool as she spied Ethan standing in the doorway. "When did you get here?" she asked, more sharply than she intended.

He looked insulted. "Just in time to hear that I'm not wanted."

"Oh," Denise moaned.

"Ah," Cameron said.

Joanne just laughed.

Denise turned to her, accusingly. "Did you know he was going to show up?"

"Not exactly."

"Cameron? Did you?"

"Kind of," he replied, then looked at his watch as if he had just remembered he had one. "Gosh. Look at the time. Jo, we've got to go."

Denise wasn't fooled. "Where?" she demanded.

"Spouses. You'll understand one day," Joanne said with a smirk.

Before Denise could even think of a sharp retort, they were gone, leaving Denise to stand there next to Ethan. "Look, I'm sorry. Cameron and Joanne love to tease me. Sometimes I just kind of snap."

He didn't take the hint and leave it alone. "Your mom and dad used to talk about you a lot. Didn't you have a pretty serious boyfriend?"

"Yes, well, I was pretty serious. He was serious about his career."

"I'm sorry."

Denise eyed him closely, checking for a sardonic gleam or a hint of his smile. Was he being sincere? Or just playing with her feelings? "Me too," she said, noticing that they were now completely alone. "What's up?"

"I was hoping I'd find you. I've got a couple of guys who offered to help me work the next three days . . . twelve to fifteen hours a day. I thought I better warn you."

"That's great!"

"Yeah. I think we'll be able to have you moved in right on schedule."

"When you mentioned that at the dinner I was afraid to get my hopes up."

"Go ahead and get your hopes up. So, is the large work crew okay? It's going to make my estimate for labor go up."

"That's better than okay. Thank you."

"No problem."

Standing there, next to him, made her feel his presence even more than she usually did. He smelled like soap and mint. His body was solid and muscular, far more muscular than Chad's lithe body had ever been.

Denise knew for a fact that Ethan wasn't the kind of guy to run on treadmills or lift weights three times a week, either.

No, his physique came from old-fashioned hard work—hours in his store, in the lumber yards, and doing construction outside. He was so solid, he looked like he could handle any situation.

He coughed.

Shoot! She'd been staring at him! "Sorry. I guess my mind was just drifting."

"That's okay. Mine was too." With a teasing glint, he said softly, "Want to share?"

Was he flirting? "Not especially."

"I'm not, you know."

"You're not what?"

"I'm not 'almost engaged' to anyone. Rachel and I have just been dating."

Oh, he had heard their whole conversation! Lying through her teeth, she said, "Rachel is a nice girl." If a person was into barracudas.

"Really? I kind of got the feeling you two didn't like each other."

"Oh, I wouldn't say that. Rachel and I were on the same cheer squad in high school. We were up for the same award, and it created a lot of bad feelings." Just hearing herself talk about something that had happened almost ten years before embarrassed her. "Sorry. It's one of those dumb high school stories that won't ever die."

Ethan sat down on the stool Cameron had just vacated. "So . . . who got the award?"

"It's not important. All that matters now is our future."

"Hey, I was in high school once. I'm interested."

For some reason, Denise believed him, and then she sat down across from him. "I did," she finally admitted. "I got an award and my picture in the paper and a savings bond for college. And my family—being my family—made a big deal about it." The memory of it all made her cringe. "Rachel's mom kind of made a stink. Poor Rachel had to deal with that."

Surprise, and more than a little respect, entered his eyes. "You felt bad, didn't you?"

Had she? "I wouldn't necessarily say I felt bad, but I did feel uncomfortable. I loved getting the award, but my family would have taken me out to dinner because I got second place too. Rachel's mom made her feel so bad; a lot of people felt sorry for her. And then there's the whole college thing. I think she feels that I had every opportunity to do something great, and I haven't yet."

"Hey, at least you got to go. You studied history, right?"

"Yep. Well, for one year." Thinking about his hard work, she said, "I heard you're doing well in college."

"Yeah, I am. I'm taking classes in math and architecture." He bent his head down, as if he were embarrassed. "Both of my parents were happy to finish high school; they never wanted or needed college. My sister

Lindsay earned scholarships and got a degree. I just went straight to work. But now, knowing how much I like designing things . . . one day I want to be able to say I have a degree too." He shrugged. "Your dad was one of the first people who helped me see that it could actually happen. I owe a lot to your parents."

Denise reached out and squeezed his hand. "They like you."

He clasped hers right back, making her pulse race. "You want to know a secret?"

"Of course."

"You're a good person, Denise Reece."

This time, she felt like ducking her head. "You hardly know me."

"I've heard a lot of stories about you. And I'm a pretty good judge of character. I like how you haven't let what happened in California break you down. I'm glad you care enough about the theater to try and revitalize it." He lowered his voice. "I like how you're not perfect."

"I'm far from that."

"Me too."

His statement, so honestly spoken, made her meet his gaze. "Thanks for helping me with the theater."

"You're welcome."

She swallowed as their hands parted, though a new awareness had formed between them, making Denise realize that she was definitely not immune to Ethan Flynn, not in any shape or form.

Ethan cleared his throat. "Are you ready to go through some of these designs for the theater's foyer?"

"Of course," she said, hoping her voice sounded more business-like than she felt. "I wrote down some ideas I had last night. Perhaps we could—"

A crash sounded on the bottom floor.

Denise flinched. "What do you think that was?"

"I don't know. Maybe the ghost?" Ethan said with a hint of a smile.

She didn't know whether to grab his arm for security or hit him in frustration.

Fear won. Clutching his arm, she said, "What do you think we should do?"

He covered her hand with his own. "Go check things out. Come on."

Together, they trudged down the stairs, Ethan holding her hand tightly. As they carefully navigated the creaking stairs, Denise was well aware that her heart was beating wildly and her imagination was reeling out of control.

All the reading she'd done about ghostly visits and hauntings raced through her head, making her wary of each creak in the staircase.

As if he had read her mind, Ethan squeezed her hand, bringing warmth and security in his weathered palm. "You okay?"

Denise could only nod as a mixture of emotions rolled through her. Slowly they descended, but as they came to the main room, they found the culprit—a fallen ladder.

Ethan, still clasping her hand, drew her attention to a window in the far corner of the room. The pane had been raised a good four inches.

"Window's open," he said. "I guess the wind blew the ladder down."

It hadn't been open earlier. "Who do you think did that?" she asked, a strange sense of foreboding filtering through her.

"No telling." Then, as if he just realized their hands were still clasped, he dropped his quickly. "Maybe it really was open and you didn't realize it."

She would have realized it. The window was large, almost four feet wide. Even when it was open a crack, a good sized breeze blew through it.

But as she flexed her now empty hand, and felt his emotional withdrawal as well, she knew better than to say anything. He'd probably think she was crazy if she insisted the place was haunted.

At the moment, she felt completely alone, chilled, and confused about the crazy thoughts running through her head—ghosts, windows, family . . . and Ethan's strong, warm hands and firm frame standing close beside her.

Ethan stepped away. "I better get going," he said, not giving a reason, but Denise knew why.

There was too much between them. Too much unspoken.

But even if they could never fall in love, she knew they'd just reached a turning point in their relationship.

Friends.

They were a lot alike, and she trusted him.

The thought was so jarring, her mind practically rang as she calculated her feelings.

She trusted him because he was a good person. Sincere. As opposite from Chad and his Teflon smile as night and day.

He was like another brother, though Lord knew she didn't need any more.

"Thanks for everything," she whispered.

Ethan stepped back from the window he'd just shut and caught her eye. "No problem," he said.

"I'll try to stay out of your way when you're working."

His gaze held her own. "No reason to, it's your place."

"You won't mind if I came by a couple of times a day?"

"I'd be surprised if you didn't," he said, then waved goodbye.

As Denise watched him leave, a strange part of her hoped he was on his way to see Rachel. A part of her hoped that Rachel would have dinner or pizza or something ready for him and that they could spend the evening enjoying each other's company, like she used to do with Chad.

No, scratch that. Like she'd used to do with her brothers and Joanne.

Chapter Six

The next few days passed in a whirlwind. Though Denise was busy with the architect, legal issues, and research about Sally's past, the majority of her time was spent with her mom.

Together, they went on shopping trips and to matinees. They talked and drank coffee and ate cookies that they claimed they shouldn't but tasted good. And, as their relationship evolved from merely mother-daughter to friends, Denise realized they were forming new bonds, not just ones based on the past.

Every time her mom asked her opinions about curtains or casseroles or her siblings, Denise felt more connected than she had in years.

She was learning that her mother was a pretty smart woman.

Daphne Reece, under her designer outfits and carefully polished toenails, had an incredibly giving heart and an instinct for relationships that Denise hadn't inherited.

She listened carefully as her mom shared thoughts and feelings about each of her siblings' forays into love and marriage. And she did her best to ignore her mother's sly attempts at matchmaking.

Through it all, she saw Ethan at least twice a day. He was constantly busy, either working at his store, studying for his class, or making her apartment into something special. More than once she found him hot and sweaty, bent over a windowpane or under a kitchen counter.

Just that morning, she'd walked into her apartment to find him installing a new cabinet in the bathroom. The sight of him, crouched under the sink, shirt untucked, muscles straining, made her heart skip.

Not good. She'd decided to keep her distance from him, both emotionally and physically. He had Rachel. End of story.

Of course, she hadn't come up with a plan of what to do when they were sharing a bathroom.

She played it safe by gripping the doorjamb. "Ethan. Hi."

As he unbent from his pretzeled position and caught sight of her, his face lit up. "Well, if it isn't my lovely boss."

Ethan's hair was tousled and just a little bit damp,

kind of the way she imagined he'd look when he woke up in the morning.

She swallowed hard.

Rachel. Rachel Penderton, she reminded herself. "I'm not technically your boss," she protested.

"You're paying the bills. To me, that's one and the same." From his crouch, he waved a hand toward the new sink and bathtub. "So, what do you think?"

With extreme will, she forced herself to look at the fixtures. "I think it looks great."

"That's it? Great?" he teased. "I've practically contorted myself into a hundred unnamed positions and that's the best you can do?"

Playing along, she shook her head. "I could probably do better."

"Go ahead."

His teasing made her smile inside. Trying for levity, she said, "I like the tile?"

"There's nothing special about the tile." He pressed. "What about the tub?"

The tub, constructed of cast iron and sporting four clawed feet, looked exactly like the one she'd circled in the catalog during a previous meeting. "I adore it," she said. "I can't believe you were able to get it up here."

"We used a pulley system and hoisted it through the window."

"That's impressive." She sneaked another glance at him. Actually, it was Ethan who was impressive. Clad in a snug grayish-white T-shirt and faded jeans, he looked like he just stepped out of a magazine's photo spread.

He motioned over her shoulder. "And the kitchen sink? What did you think about that?"

Actually, plumbing and fixtures were the last things on her mind. "It's great too."

Ethan laughed as he stood up. "Ha! I had a feeling you weren't looking around very carefully. My partner Jeff and I haven't put the kitchen sink in, yet." He stepped forward. "But I'll show you what we have done. Got a minute to look around?"

She swallowed. "Sure."

With a smile, Ethan began his tour. Never had her tiny apartment felt so confining. Denise was aware of each step and each motion of the man next to her and especially the way his gaze seemed to hold hers just a second too long, or how his shoulder rubbed against her own just a bit too much.

How easily she could imagine being in a relationship with him. How easily she could see herself looking forward to getting off work just to receive his warm smile and a comforting hug.

Maybe even a tender kiss.

"Now, here, I know you were wanting to put in an entertainment center, but Jeff and I were talking, and I think we should just build you one," Ethan said from the corner of her new living room. "Then, there would be room for a small loveseat in the corner. What do you think?"

Denise scanned the area and did her best not to think about love seats and Ethan Flynn. "That sounds great."

He tilted his head. " 'Great' how? 'Great' to the love seat or 'great' to the built-in cabinet?"

What had he said about a cabinet? All Denise could think about was how cute he looked in his worn construction boots.

Gosh, was she looking at his feet?

"I think everything sounds 'great,' " she said quickly. "I'm really impressed with your work, and how fast everything has come together."

White teeth flashed as he grinned. "Thanks. It's been fun. Jeff and I were thinking that we've kind of liked the challenges of working in such a small space. We might even start making it our specialty when we start advertising for more work."

"From the looks of everything, I think you should," she said.

Ethan stepped forward. "I'm glad. I'm glad you're happy with everything. I would have been disappointed if you weren't."

The faint scent of his cologne tickled her nose. "I'm not disappointed at all," she murmured, finally giving into the pleasure of being completely alone with him, of being on the receiving end of that warm gaze and that sexy smile. "In fact, I'm pretty—"

Thankfully, the cell phone that was clipped on his

belt rang, interrupting any embarrassing words that were forthcoming.

"Hold that thought," he said, as he reached for the phone.

She needed to get a hold of herself, to reestablish a working relationship. She had to keep her focus on the apartment and not Ethan. She took a good two steps back, just to be on the safe side.

"Flynn," he said into the phone.

Denise watched as his expression turned startled, then strained. "Hey," he said, turning away from her.

She had a very good idea of who was on the line. Rachel.

Like ice water hitting her face, Denise felt her insides wake up and beg for reprieve, but it was impossible not to stand there and listen.

"No. I'm still working. Theater."

Ethan stepped away, as if he was distancing himself physically as well as mentally. She felt his absence just as intensely.

He treated her to a brief glance before speaking again. "I'm not sure. Lunch?"

Their former friendly coziness now felt shameful. Too close. Obtrusive. Wrong.

Since the room was so small, there was only one thing to do to get relief. "I'm just going to leave," she mouthed to him when he glanced her way again.

He held up a finger, signaling her to wait.

She edged toward the stairs but didn't go down.

Obviously, Rachel continued to talk in his ear. Stress replaced the earlier teasing sparkle of his eyes. His left hand squeezed the windowsill.

Denise felt sorry for him until she realized that there was nothing to feel sorry about. Rachel Penderton was Ethan Flynn's girlfriend. She had his cell phone number and had every right to make cozy lunch dates with him.

He obviously loved her, or at least liked her very much or he wouldn't be with her. And from what her family had insinuated, they'd been together for several months. They had a relationship.

Just like she used to have. Just like the one she'd told herself she didn't want to have again for a very long time. She had enough on her plate without romance, no matter what her pulse did whenever Ethan was around.

It was almost easy to take the first step down on the stairs.

Ethan clicked off. "Sorry," he said. "Rachel—"

This time, she held up a finger. "You don't need to apologize."

He shook his head. "She doesn't seem to understand—"

Denise cut him off again. She was pretty sure Rachel understood everything just fine. "I think it's best I leave. I'll stop by again in a few days."

He blinked. "But don't you want to see everything else?"

Remembering how she'd been far more taken with

his muscular build than anything else, she shook her head. "I think . . . I've seen enough. I better go."

As she hurried down the steps and opened the door to the main part of the building, Denise tried to not mind that Ethan didn't follow her.

Chapter Seven

"So then, Mrs. Jackson said, 'I'll only redecorate my living room if Rachel is in charge!'" Rachel paused dramatically as if she were waiting for the statement to sink in.

He did his best to nod in complete understanding.

She continued. "Why, I could have just about died! Ethan, do you know what a big deal that recommendation is?" Rachel squeezed his arm possessively.

Ethan fought to keep his temper in check. Not only was the blood slowing in his arm from her firm grip, but she had developed an annoying habit of speaking to him as if he were a child. They both knew he was far from that. Once again, he wondered how much longer he was going to try to keep their relationship going.

In the past, her possessiveness had amused him. Now

he only felt trapped. "I do," he finally stated, when it looked as if they'd get no farther without some effort on his part.

Rachel shook her head. "I don't think you really do. Mrs. Jackson is, like, the pillar in the community. If she gives me the stamp of approval, then I'll have it made! I might even get my name listed on the company letter-head! Maybe one day I'll even be a partner."

"Wow." He hadn't known decorating was so cut-throat. Actually he hadn't known a lot of things about Rachel's world before they had started dating.

"Wow is right." She squeezed his arm again as they walked toward the country club house. "I'm so glad you agreed to come here with me."

"No problem," he lied. Ethan didn't want to be there. Pizza or burgers were more his style than fancy food and the jacket and tie he sported. While he didn't mind dressing up every once in a while, he felt out of place and uncomfortable at the country club.

Rachel knew this, but didn't care. It had ticked him off at first, but when he calmed down, he'd realized it was all part of the deal. Doing things you didn't want to do was part of any relationship. And besides, he was in love, right?

Love.

Was he in love?

No.

Had he ever been?

Rachel smiled brightly, her cheeks glowing pink in

the dim light. "I just didn't want to celebrate all alone."

There were a thousand other places they could have gone, and at any of those places, they would have been together. He almost reminded her of that fact.

But it wasn't his night. "This is fine."

"My parents said they might stop by if their previous engagement ends early." She tilted her head up to meet his eyes. "They'd love to see you, by the way. I'm sure they're going to want to ask you all about work and about your college classes. It's going to be so awesome when you finally get your degree."

Ethan strived for patience. He knew Rachel was just voicing his own thoughts. And, truthfully, he loved talking about his job and was proud of the work he was doing. The renovations he and Jeff had done so far could hold their own against any big name companies in town. "I'll tell them about the theater."

Rachel turned to him in surprise. "You mean . . . Denise Reece's theater?"

Was there any other? "Well, yeah," he said, unable to soften his tone. Hadn't she been paying any attention to him during the last few days? All he'd talked about was the work on the apartment.

Rachel squeezed his arm again. A little harder than necessary. "Oh, don't mention that, would you, Ethan?"

"Why not?"

"My family never has cared much for hers. And besides, there's not really much to tell about that theater, anyway. I mean, it's not like anyone is about to perform there."

Actually, he was pretty sure people *were* planning to perform there. And, he, personally, thought it was a pretty great addition to the town. It was also a great opportunity for him, professionally, and he wanted to talk about it.

But, it was Rachel's night. He gritted his teeth. One night in the future would be his. "I won't mention a thing."

"Thank you," she said, and gave him a little kiss on the cheek as a reward.

For some reason, that gesture really irked him. Rachel had a habit of depositing affection for good behavior. Wickedly, Ethan wondered what she'd do if he grabbed her and kissed her hard, without reason.

He was pretty sure she wouldn't be happy about it. Of course, he was pretty certain he wouldn't be happy about it, either.

He needed to end their relationship. He should have done it two weeks ago, when he'd dreamed of Denise. He'd just been afraid to rush into another relationship . . . especially with someone he hadn't been sure he even liked.

But now he knew for certain that he liked Denise very much. Probably too much.

As Rachel slipped her perfectly matched purse over her shoulder, she paused so he could open the door for her.

The place was crowded. Lots of noisy men and women, milling around. Ethan recognized most of the people. Everyone had been in his store at one time or another.

Rachel was in her element, clasping his hand, and chatting with everyone. Though several did stop and ask how he was doing, Ethan rarely had a chance to reply. Rachel was excited about her compliment and was unable to focus on anything else.

Once, he would have found her childish excitement endearing. Now, he found it more than a little trying. He resented her need for attention, as well as her assumption that he would have little to say to the members of the club.

"Two, tonight?" Payton Chase, the manager of the club asked. Ethan knew him from his visits to the hardware store and the bike path. They both shared a love for thirty mile rides.

"Hey, Payton," Ethan said. "What are you doing, seating us?"

"Charlie called in sick. You know how it is."

"I do. Just the other day, Al—"

"Two, please, Payton. And could you put us over by the McKinneys?"

Payton looked at Rachel in surprise and then, just because he could, said, "What was that, Ethan?"

Ethan stifled a grin. "Nothing. Just that Allen called in sick the other day. Ended up working thirteen hours at the store."

Payton looked like he was tempted to add more, but he went ahead and walked them to the nearest vacant table. "This is going to have to do, Rachel. Busy night tonight."

Rachel merely pursed her lips.

Ethan had had enough. "What's going on with you?" he asked as soon as Payton had left them. "All night you've acted as if you're more important than me, or anyone else in the room."

Instantly, she looked contrite. "I'm sorry. I guess I was just a little too full of myself and so eager to build on my success. My father spent many a night in here establishing contacts. It's one of the best reasons to join."

Ethan was going to say something about that but knew there wasn't a thing he could say that wouldn't touch off yet another argument. Instead, he scanned over the menu and the room as well.

There, in the back corner, sat Denise Reece with Kevin, Missy, their baby, and her parents. As if on cue, she looked up and caught his eye and smiled.

Rachel caught the exchange, too. "Of all the nights to be here. It's bad enough I had to deal with Payton Chase. But now Denise too." She scanned the tables. "And I don't even see my parents. They thought they might be able to get here by seven."

After the waiter brought them tea and they ordered, Ethan did his best to concentrate on what Rachel was saying. But it was hard. He could tell she'd merely used him as an escort, as someone to sit with until she saw other people who mattered. And now that he obviously wasn't going to praise her success any longer, she was chafing to go talk to other people.

Quite honestly, he was eager for her to go.

"Why don't you go say hi to the McKinneys," he finally suggested.

Her eyes widened. "You don't mind?"

Ethan knew it would be a relief. "Not at all."

Without any further prodding, Rachel left and, with a bright smile, began circulating the room.

It gave Ethan plenty of time to think about their relationship. It had been strictly casual for most of the time. Only recently had it threatened to become a real relationship. Actually, only after he'd been written up in the *Payton Registrar* for one of his jobs for the historical society.

Most of the time, he felt completely self-assured; he didn't know how to act otherwise. But lately, it seemed that Rachel thrived on pointing their differences out— their different backgrounds, his lack of schooling, his love of fishing and biking, and the way he could care less about designer tags.

He glanced toward Rachel again. She had now joined another table and was pulling out a business card. He did have to hand it to the girl; she was nothing if not tenacious.

Their food came. He went ahead and started eating.

In fact, he was half-way through when he looked up to see Mr. Reece approaching.

"Ethan Flynn," he said. "Come on over and join us."

He gestured over to Rachel. "Well, I . . ."

Jim waved a hand in dismissal, effectively cutting off any excuses. "She's talking draperies with half those women. Haven't you noticed everyone's playing musical chairs?"

Ethan finally did take a moment to take notice of where everyone was. Rachel now sat with a trio of women. Their husbands were having burgers and playing cards by the fireplace. Several other people had pulled up chairs to a back table and were watching sports highlights.

"Come on, Ethan. No reason for you to be sitting by your lonesome."

And with that, Ethan picked up his plate and brought it over to the Reece table. "Hey," he said to everyone before finally meeting Denise's eyes.

"Glad you could join us," she said.

He wasn't sure if she meant it or not. All he did know was that the Reece family looked genuinely happy to see him. "Me too," he said, knowing he meant it. His shoulders relaxed as he became engulfed in their happy chatter.

Chapter Eight

Denise couldn't believe Ethan was sitting with them, and Rachel didn't even notice he was gone. Honestly, if Ethan had been her boyfriend, she would have kept tabs on him at all times. There was no telling who would be on the prowl for such a good-looking, easy-going guy.

She swallowed hard. Obviously, someone like her!

Not that she was looking. She wasn't on the rebound. She wasn't. Really.

"You okay?" he asked.

"Of course. I, uh, was just wondering if you're worried about Rachel."

Ethan turned around and looked for her. After a minute, he faced Denise again. "I think she's pretty well set up with some prospective clients."

It looked to Denise like Rachel was ignoring him.

As if he felt the need to explain further, Ethan added, "She got some great news today. You know how it is."

"Oh, sure." Rachel's antics made her think of Chad and how he'd seen every party as a chance to network. He'd been great at self-promotion and horrible at thinking of her needs.

More than ever, Denise was starting to feel very grateful Chad had broken up with her. Sometimes, things really did work out for the best.

Eager to break the awkward silence, she cleared her throat and asked, "So, how's the work coming on the apartment?"

"So far, so good. We got a lot done yesterday, and there's a crew coming in early tomorrow morning." He gave Denise a smile. "Plan to be living on your own by the end of next week."

Daphne Reece gasped as she leaned forward and entered the conversation. "So soon? Ethan, your crew is amazing."

"Things are going well."

"Yes they are." A worried line appeared between her brows. "Of course, I just don't know what we're going to do without Denise at home."

Denise's eyes lit with humor. "Mom, I've only been back two months."

"I know, but we've had so much fun."

Amazingly, they had. "We'll still see each other."

"I know. I just didn't expect things to happen so quickly," Daphne explained to Ethan. "Oh my gosh!"

she exclaimed. "Denise, you've got to find a theater director. We better get something in the papers before long, or you won't be able to produce a play for months."

Denise felt the same way. Things were happening so quickly, she felt she was constantly rushing to keep up. "I know, it's just that it's going to be tricky."

Ethan turned to her. "Why's that?"

"Well, it's got to be someone who won't mind starting from scratch, and who won't mind me being in the middle of it all. A lot of people wouldn't want to work so closely with someone who doesn't have a theater background."

The talk about specifics made her recall all the paperwork she had painstakingly read the night before. "Dad, I looked over the documents from Aunt Flo again last night. I'm going to need your help with them."

Jim Reece nodded. "We'll do that first thing next week."

As they discussed that, Ethan finished his meal and ordered coffee. All the while, an idea began formulating in his head. "My sister Lindsay might be perfect for the job. She majored in performing arts."

Everyone's head turned in his direction. "Really?" Denise asked. "Do you think she might be interested in the theater?"

"I think she *really* might be interested."

"Are you sure? It's not going to be very professional. Don't you think she might be looking for a bigger venue to showcase her talents?"

"No. She's not like that. She's young, and small town at heart."

"But you think she would know how to create a theater company?"

"She's been in more plays than I can count. She's done everything from acting to stage work to spotlights to directing."

Her parents gave her a meaningful look.

"She sounds perfect," her dad said.

"Completely perfect, don't you think?" her mom asked. Denise was feeling too much relief to care that they were pushing.

"Would you mind giving her a call to see if she would be interested in helping with the theater? That is, if she doesn't mind a few ghosts roaming around," she added, thinking how spooked she'd been when that ladder had fallen.

"Lindsay's pretty tough. I don't know if anything scares her."

Jim chuckled. "Not even a bunch of people on the steering committee?"

"Now that might present a problem," Ethan quipped.

Denise couldn't help but smile as well. It was true; sometimes the scariest part about reclaiming the theater was getting along with so many divergent personalities. As Cam and Joanne had predicted, everyone was ready to be in charge. But, for the first time, Denise was more than ready to accept all their help and advice.

The conversation flowed from there, and Denise felt her shoulders relax as they began to joke about the many interesting personalities in Payton.

They talked about Payton Chase, the manager of the country club, and Priscilla, his wife, who was the club's chef. Both were type-A personalities and they constantly bickered.

The conversation then shifted to the family, Ethan's sister, and then the mayor.

Denise had no problem completely forgetting all about Rachel Penderton or that Ethan was supposedly very close to her until Rachel came over and squeezed Ethan's shoulder.

"Ethan, what exactly are you doing over here?"

All conversation stopped.

"Rachel." His tone was practically frigid. With concise movements, he scooted back, forcing Rachel to drop her hand.

Denise had never heard him sound so angry and tired all at once. She caught her parents' eyes. They had a look on their faces that suggested they did not appreciate being treated like soldiers in an enemy camp.

But Ethan didn't look surprised or even embarrassed by Rachel's appearance. If anything, he looked kind of relieved that she was making such a scene. "I'm drinking coffee, Rachel," he said, finally answering her question.

"Why are you sitting here? I looked up and saw that you had left me!"

"No. We both know that is not how it happened. You left me to go sit with the McKinneys. I was sitting alone. Jim invited me to join them."

"Would you care to join us too?" Jim Reece asked. Missy moved closer to Kevin to make room for another chair.

"No, I do not." Raising her chin, Rachel said, "Ethan, I'm ready to go."

"You're going to have to wait. I was about to order dessert."

This was news to Denise, though she knew to keep her mouth shut. By the looks from everyone else, they were doing the same.

One more time, her dad said, "Rachel, why don't you join us? There's no need for you to be standing here," he added pointedly.

She directed a particularly nasty look Denise's way. "No, thank you."

The whole atmosphere in the club stilled as Rachel's poor behavior caused more notice. Several tables stopped conversation altogether, and more than one person looked ready to guide Rachel out of there.

But for once, Rachel didn't look ready to accept any assistance. "I'm telling you, Ethan Flynn, if you stay here with Denise and her family, our relationship is finished."

Ethan narrowed his eyes. "I'll be sorry that you'll want to end it that way."

Denise couldn't help but notice Ethan didn't say that he'd be sorry to break up. She couldn't help but feel happy about that though she knew she should be feeling sorry for Ethan.

Payton Chase stepped forward, obviously ready to either pull over a chair or to guide Rachel out. Anything to ease the tense situation and restore calm.

Rachel inhaled deeply.

Denise held her breath for the torrent of words that was about to break from Rachel.

She wasn't disappointed. "Ethan Flynn, we are through! I can't believe you have the nerve to treat me so shabbily. And you, Denise Reece, I can't believe you had the nerve to come back to Payton and steal my boyfriend." Then she stomped her foot. "One day, you're going to feel really ashamed of yourself. And one day, you're going to wish that you treated me better. Both of you!"

And with that, she turned on her heel and left the building.

Denise stared at her parents in shock.

Kevin coughed.

Missy patted Tam, her baby.

The rest of the dining room watched Rachel leave before murmuring among themselves.

Payton stepped forward, looking like he was about to say something, and then finally decided to retreat as well.

Jim Reece took a lengthy sip of his drink. "Ethan,

your love life is your business, but I have to say, you're better off without her."

"I've never seen such a scene!" her mother added. "And to think I introduced her to Marianne McKinney! I'm going to be sure and tell her no custom-made curtains are worth that kind of behavior."

Still Ethan said nothing. He looked rather shaken, and more than a little shocked.

Denise felt her resolve to keep herself distant from him melt away. "I'm sorry, Ethan," she said. "I don't know what I did to make her so mad at me, but I never intended to hurt your relationship."

Finally, he looked at her. "You didn't. We've been having trouble for some time. Rachel is a very insecure person."

Mrs. Reece reached out and squeezed Denise's hand. "Don't worry, honey. I'm sure Rachel will soon realize what a mess she's made of everything and apologize."

"Maybe, maybe not," Denise said. "She's pretty much just accused me of setting out to steal her boyfriend. People don't change their minds about that kind of thing very easily."

"They do if it's not true."

Denise knew her mother had a point. And, because she still remembered the whole range of emotions she felt during her breakup with Chad, from hurt to anger to dismay, she felt almost philosophical. "I guess now I realize how that Sally girl must have felt all those years ago. It's hard to be judged for things I never did. To apologize for things I never said."

"I'll talk to her," Ethan said.

"No," Daphne interjected, surprising Denise. "That's what Rachel wants, Ethan. She wants you to run after her. Stay here with us and have your coffee."

He looked at her in surprise. "You know, I never did order dessert."

"I know."

They looked up as Payton Chase came forward. "Ever get the feeling that your life is a soap opera?" he asked with a wry smile. "That woman could give more than a few Hollywood actresses a run for their money."

"Sorry about all this," Ethan said.

"Why? Life happens!" He held out some menus. "How about some dessert? Priscilla made some great pies and cakes tonight."

"I'd love a piece of that chocolate pecan pie," Jim Reece said.

"And coffee!" Daphne proclaimed. "Coffee for everyone!"

Ethan nodded, then finally stood up. "Thanks, but I think I'm going to call it a night." Fumbling in his pocket, he pulled out his wallet. "I'll take care of my bill with Payton before I go."

And with that, he walked away, making Denise feel relieved, sorry, and more than a little disturbed.

Because inside, she was really, really happy that Ethan was now available.

Chapter Nine

The next few days were draining, to say the least. Ethan divided his time between the store, theater renovations, and reliving Rachel's theatrics at the country club.

Practically everyone in Payton seemed to have made time to stop by the hardware store and give their two cents regarding the break-up.

More than once he'd been caught off-guard by people asking for nails, electrical cord, and more information about that fateful night. He'd done his best to help them find the supplies and then change the subject.

At least business was good.

It was almost comical that his reputation was now defined by Rachel's parting words in the middle of the country club, especially since he had worked so hard to be thought of as dependable and trustworthy, and especially since he'd never belonged to a country club in his life.

Now he was known as the guy who'd stood up to Rachel Penderton in front of Payton's high society and had lived to tell about it. It turned out that a lot of people had never been real fans of her high-handed ways. Too bad no one had ever told him that before he'd dated her for six months.

For a reason Ethan couldn't fathom, he wasn't even terribly mad at Rachel for being so vindictive. No, on the contrary, he felt sorry for her, and, he was secretly relieved that their relationship had ended. During the last several days, he hadn't been able to stop thinking of Denise, yet he also hadn't been able to think of a way of breaking it off with Rachel without hurting her feelings in the process.

But now, he'd managed to do that anyway. The latest gossip was that Rachel was still as mad as could be and was making a voodoo doll of him in front of her friends. He was fine with that. Well, as fine as he could be with someone completely trashing his reputation.

The only thing he really regretted about the whole incident was that Denise had witnessed it. He'd seen her appalled expression during Rachel's rant and was sure it was yet another reason she wished he'd never attached himself to her family. Even though he knew he'd been right to break up with Rachel, he also worried that Denise now would never want to be involved with him. Nobody wanted to be around someone with loads of emotional baggage.

Ironically though, since the break-up, he had felt as if a huge load had been lifted from his shoulders. Now he was free to think about a certain blonde beauty named Denise Rose Reece. From the start, she'd captured his attention with her pretty ways and her shy, uncertain demeanor, but he'd forced himself to ignore his feelings.

Now that he and Rachel were history, he couldn't help but think about Denise again and wonder if they could ever have a future together.

He was still pondering it all when his sister Lindsay called him back on Wednesday night.

"What's this I hear about a new theater that's looking for a manager?" she asked in that no-frills way of hers. "Mom and Dad told me all about your project when we had dinner last week."

"Are you interested?"

"Definitely."

As succinctly as possible, he told her about the theater, Denise's plans for it, and his remodeling work.

Finally, he paused. "So Lindsay, what do you think? Will you consider visiting Payton this weekend?"

"Gosh, I don't know," she replied, her voice becoming playful on the other end of the line. "Hmm. I could either stay home by myself, waiting for a Broadway producer to call, or I could visit you and consider the opportunity to manage my very own theater. It sounds like it's going to be a tough decision. I may have to get back to you on that."

He laughed. "I guess it's not much of a decision, huh?"

"Nope. It's an opportunity of a lifetime," she said, her voice uncharacteristically quiet. "Thanks for mentioning me to your friend."

"No problem. You'd be great at this; we both know that. And besides, I'd love to have you in Payton."

"I'd like being closer to you too. So, what's the owner like? Do you think I should come with a resumé and business plan? Should I go buy a new suit?" The last was asked a little frantically. It was obvious that his sister was pretty nervous.

Thinking about Lindsay wandering around Payton in a suit made him smile. His sister favored jeans and t-shirts as much as he did. And, for some reason, he couldn't imagine Denise worrying about fancy outfits, either. "The owner is new to all this, like I said. She's not the kind of person to judge you by what you're wearing. I don't think you'll need to wear a suit."

"What's she like, Ethan?" Lindsay repeated. "Details, please."

Now, *that* was a typical Lindsay response. He smiled as he thought of his younger sister, probably sitting on her couch, papers surrounding her, an old pencil and notebook perched on her lap.

"Details? Hmm." How could he describe a woman

he was still trying to figure out? "Let's see. She's young. About in her mid-twenties. Pretty."

He could hear the faint tapping of a pencil. "And?"

Numerous adjectives filled his mind, but none seemed to completely describe her complex personality completely. "She's kind of skittish," he finally said. "She seems to worry about things more than I ever thought she would. This whole theater thing kind of took her by surprise. But, she's trying hard." He thought some more. "She's loyal to her family."

"She's a Reece, right?"

"Yep."

"Does she know how much you admire her parents? Some people get weird when they know other people are close to their family."

"I think at first it took her by surprise, but now I don't think it bothers her at all. She seems to admire them. You'll like Jim and Daphne Reece too, Lindsay. They're great. She is too," he added, with some surprise. Just listening to himself made Ethan realize that he'd thought far more about Denise, her family, and his relationship with them than he had realized.

"Well, I'm going to be a nervous wreck, but I'm going to take you and Denise up on the invitation."

"I knew you weren't going to need days to think it over."

"That's not my style."

"No, it's not," he agreed, thinking that as long as he could remember, Lindsay had made split-second decisions. He was the one who worried and waited and thought about ramifications.

Just thinking about consequences reminded him of something else. "Um, there's something else that you might want to be aware of."

"What's that?"

"This theater is supposed to be haunted."

She burst out laughing.

"I'm being completely serious," he said, even though he knew it sounded crazy. He was the last person to take a haunted house seriously.

When Lindsay caught her breath, she asked, "Have you seen anything yet?"

"Well, no, not really, though Denise and I once thought a window opened mysteriously. Then there's the fact that the crew says someone keeps turning on the boom box at eight o'clock every night."

"Well, at least the ghost has a sense of humor," she quipped. "Maybe she likes to dance."

"Ha, ha." Ethan frowned. "I'm serious about this ghost thing," he said again. "There's supposed to be the spirit of some jilted gal floating around the place. She may give you some trouble."

He held the phone away from his ear as she laughed once again. "You're acting like something could actually happen!" she said when she caught her breath.

He felt his cheeks heating. "It might. I'm telling you this because there's a chance that you could be getting more than you bargained for. All I know is that more than one person believes it's haunted," he added. "It's one of the reasons no one has done anything with the old place."

"Well, there's got to be an angle that we can use. We're just going to have to make that ghost work for us," she added, tapping her pencil again. "Maybe—if I get hired—we could do something around that, like perform a mystery for opening night. Every place needs a hook."

He was no expert on that. There was a reason he was in hardware. "Ghosts sound hook-worthy."

"What does this Denise gal think?"

"I think she's more worried about the ghost's reputation than business," he said honestly. "For some reason, Denise thinks she has a responsibility to clear the ghost's name."

Lindsay chuckled. "I can't wait to meet her."

"I can't wait for you to, either. When I first saw Denise, I couldn't believe how pretty she was. I mean, her blonde hair is really thick," he said, picturing how she looked the last time they were at the theater together. "It falls in waves almost to her shoulder blades. Gray eyes. Sculpted cheek bones. And—"

"Cut!" Lindsay said. "Hello? Ethan, are you sure you're *Ethan Flynn*? I've never heard you gush so much about anything."

"I don't gush," he said automatically, though he had to admit that he had gotten a little carried away.

"Um, what about the infamous Rachel?"

"Infamous? You didn't like her either?" Had he been the only person in his circle of family and friends who hadn't seen her for who she was?

"Nope, and I never even met her. I just hated how you always acted like you were on her schedule. It never seemed to be the other way around."

That was because it never had been the other way around. "Why didn't you say anything?"

"It wasn't my place, and I didn't want to hurt your feelings. You liked her. That's all that mattered."

He wouldn't have minded some sisterly advice, though. "Well, Rachel is now history. We broke up in front of half the country club three nights ago."

"Ouch."

"Oh, yeah. It was one of my more embarrassing moments," he admitted, then shared the bitter details.

She whistled low when he was done. "I'll say it again. You're better off without her, Ethan. She wanted to change you."

"You know what's funny? When it all happened, I almost felt happy. I was glad she'd broken up with me and caused such a scene. Then I didn't have to feel guilty about wanting to end things with her."

He thought back to the feelings he'd had to keep bottled up inside himself after Rachel had stormed out. It had been all he could do not to shout 'hooray' and thank his lucky stars. In fact, he'd had such a hard time looking disappointed, that he'd ended up leaving abruptly to cover his tracks.

"Well, I think it's good you've already found someone else. Maybe this Denise is more your speed."

"I haven't *found* anyone. Denise and I are just friends."

"Ethan! You just got finished telling me how pretty she is!"

"Just because she's attractive doesn't mean she and I are a couple. Besides, I'm not ready to go back into a relationship."

"You don't always get to choose when you find love. Sometimes it finds you."

"Thanks for the words of wisdom."

Lindsay paused, as if she was weighing the pros and cons of badgering him. But she only said, "Well, please tell everyone I'll look forward to meeting them on Saturday."

"Will do. See you then."

After they hung up, Ethan wondered what his sister would think of Payton, Ohio. Somehow, he had a feeling that she was going to like it.

Chapter Ten

Denise decided to spend the next afternoon at the historical museum, digging up information about the theater, Sally, and Flo. Her sister Joanne, who ran the museum, was also there, eager to help, and her sister-in-law Missy was there as well, as neat and organized as usual.

Typically, Joanne arrived for their meeting with a few scribbled notes on a scratch sheet of paper, while Missy had two organized binders filled with pertinent information.

Denise had come with nothing except for a healthy respect for the two women and a need to discover the identity of the 'ghost.'

"So, I was checking around and came up with two

prevalent theories," Joanne said after they read through some news articles and got caught up.

"Which are?"

"One, there is no ghost. You've probably imagined that talcum powder scent, the window is likely broken, and some kids are probably having a good old time at your expense."

Though her head was agreeing with her sister, Denise's heart was telling her another story. "I don't think kids are doing all of this. Don't forget, I've been there when the boom box suddenly clicks on. It's creepy."

"There could be a timer or something that's triggering the radio," Joanne said, tapping the end of her pencil on the table. "You know how it is. People with nothing to do have made one up, giving them something to talk about on Sunday afternoons."

It still didn't make sense to Denise. "I don't know, Joanne. If you had seen what I had, you'd think something out of the ordinary was going on."

Missy pointed to a binder that was opened to an old news article. "What about all the sightings that have been documented over the last three decades? Joanne, Denise is not alone in this."

Joanne bit her lip. "Women with not enough to do?"

Denise drummed her fingers on the desktop in front of her. "What's the other theory?"

"Theory number two is that there really *is* a ghost, she really *is* Sally, and there's not much you can do about it. From what I've found out, it's best just to get along and not try to get rid of her. She's supposed to be relatively harmless."

"I wouldn't know how to get rid of her. I just don't want everyone to think I'm crazy," Denise said.

Missy pointed to the article again. "Oh, no one is going to think that. This binder has lots of documentation about sightings and such."

"Then why did we never hear about this ghost growing up?" Joanne asked.

"Well, it was already closed by then. And . . . Flo didn't want people to get spooked. She had enough going on with paying the building's taxes and such."

Denise could relate to that. "Now that I'm going to be paying the taxes, I can completely understand. Everything that's happened so far is pretty incredible."

Missy gazed at her outright. "You seem awfully stressed. Is there a reason you wanted to do this today? Are you worried about something?"

"No, not really. It's just that I was kind of hoping I could clear Sally's name or something."

Joanne looked at her curiously. "Why?"

Denise didn't know how to explain it. "I don't know."

"Could it be because maybe you're hoping your name will get cleared too?" Missy asked quietly.

Denise glanced at her sister-in-law and wondered once again how someone so sweet could be so blunt. "Why did you ask me that?"

"You've mentioned more than once that you've wished things had worked out better for you in California, that you wished you had been more successful, and that you could have come home a success instead of with a broken heart." She pointed to an article that told about Sally's engagement to a man named Ronald Morgan. "You and Sally have a lot in common."

"What happened to me isn't a secret."

"But the details are," Joanne said, resting her elbows on the table in front of her. "What, exactly, happened between you and Chad? I thought you were in love."

"I thought I was too." Summoning up her courage, Denise said, "We were secretly engaged. I thought I was in love. I thought we were going to get married and live in California forever. But, now . . . I realize I was just infatuated and that Chad had never even been that committed."

"Oh, Denise," Missy said.

"One day, Chad came to see me and told me that he finally got on a soap opera. I thought it meant that we were about to go out and celebrate. He meant that it was time to move on."

Joanne blinked. "End of story."

Denise tried to smile, but it was still hard. She'd felt so helpless and alone when he'd rejected her, like a complete failure. "Right. End of story."

"I bet it still hurts. You were so serious about him," Missy said.

"I thought I was. I thought we were going to

announce engaged. But now I realize that dream was way off. Chad and I had nothing in common. Now, I can see that my whole time in California was more about running away than running to anything," she admitted. "My pride was hurt more than my heart. I liked Chad, but I didn't love him. It would have been a mistake for us to get married."

Joanne touched her shoulder. "Well, I, for one, am glad you're back. You fit in here."

Denise glanced at her sister. Her touch brought back memories of being by her side when they were little, of sharing a room, of pretend tea parties, and then of Joanne blossoming in high school, winning all kinds of awards and being everyone's best friend.

Denise had felt awkward, shy, and never quite good enough. Those feelings had mushroomed into a real desire to get away instead of opening herself to her siblings and talking things out.

But now, she realized she did fit in. Joanne and Missy weren't perfect. No one in her family was.

And no one had ever expected her to be.

"Isn't that funny? I never thought I fit in," she admitted. "All of you were so busy, so involved . . . I always felt kind of lost in the shuffle."

"We weren't *that* involved. And you were too, Dee."

Thinking back to her days as a cheerleader, Denise nodded. "I guess I was."

"You're right about all of us being loud. But I think

you forgot that we all appreciated your quietness. I know Mom and Dad did. You've always had a good heart."

Denise squeezed her sister's hand. "Now things seem different. I feel as if I have a real reason to be back in Payton . . . a goal. It's good."

Joanne nodded. "I wish that we could have persuaded you to come back sooner. Then that Chad wouldn't have broken your heart."

"Doesn't Mom say that there's a reason for everything? I think that must be true, now."

"Speaking of which, maybe this whole haunted theater will work to our advantage. I think having a series of mysteries and haunted plays could become really popular."

"It's a terrific idea," Missy added.

"It's going to be a lot of work," Joanne added ominously.

"I know. I'm going to need some help," Denise admitted.

"I'm so glad to hear you say that, dear," Daphne Reece said from the doorway, along with a whole host of women.

Denise almost squealed in surprise.

Joanne did. "Mom, I didn't hear you come up the stairs."

"We were quiet. You three were obviously having an important conversation."

"A private one," Joanne muttered under her breath.

"But now we can all work on something together," Daphne said, leading in six other women.

Missy visibly worked to keep her smile in place as she stood up.

"What's going on?" Denise asked, since both her sister and sister-in-law looked to be temporarily out of words.

"We've decided to be the first performance crew."

Denise looked to Missy and Joanne for support. "Crew?"

Their mom nodded. "Yep. We're going to help put on the first play. You need help, Dee."

The rest of the women all started talking at once, each toting large canvas bags and thermoses.

By experience, Denise knew they were prepared to stay for the next four hours. "Mom, you may be rushing things. We've got to get the place cleaned up first." She thought quickly. "And the funding. I'm not sure I'm quite at the point to fund a play."

"And that's where we come in. We do great fundraisers." One of the ladies hugged Missy. "Remember your dance for the Civil War hall? We did a great job with that."

"They did," Missy agreed with a deer-in-the-headlights look.

Daphne clapped her hands, then pulled out a Tupperware container full of muffins. "Before you can say Jack Roberts, we'll have committees going for everything. You won't need to worry about a thing, Denise."

"Wow," Denise said before mouthing to Joanne, "Jack Roberts?"

Joanne shrugged.

Daphne was thrilled. "Wow, is right! Okay, everyone. Let's all take our seats. Someone give these girls an agenda."

Joanne slowly backed out of the room. "I think I better go find Stratton."

"I've got to go too," Missy said. "It's time to feed the baby. Sorry."

Denise knew for a fact that Stratton was doing hospital rounds and Missy didn't look the least bit apologetic. In fact, she looked pretty thrilled to be leaving. "Traitors," Denise whispered.

"You were in California when we went through this," Joanne whispered right back. "It's your turn."

"But . . ."

"Bye!" The two called out as they left the museum together, leaving Denise with a big group of women, two notebooks, one large agenda, and no idea how to exit gracefully.

Chapter Eleven

After an hour of being surrounded by the chatty women, Denise escaped by claiming she had an appointment with Ethan Flynn. And, because she sometimes felt as if they were all watching her, Denise trotted over to his hardware store, just so they wouldn't think she'd been lying to get out of the meeting. She had more than a few memories of being caught in a lie by her mother. It had never been a good situation.

After pushing open the door, she stepped into the old building with a sigh of relief. Finally! Peace and quiet, and no crazy women holding clipboards, fabric samples, or freshly sharpened pencils.

She was free.

Ethan looked up from his invoices. "Hey. What's going on?"

His appearance caught her by surprise, though she really wasn't sure why. It was his store. But as she caught a whiff of his tangy cologne, and noticed that he was wearing a worn denim shirt that clung to every well-formed muscle, Denise knew she really shouldn't have been surprised by the warm feeling she felt every time he was near.

Focusing on thoughts of her mom and her friends, she finally replied. "Nothing . . . everything." She stepped forward. "My mom's decided to get involved in the theater in a big way. She's formed a committee."

He grimaced. "Even I've heard about those committees."

"Believe me when I say that everything you've heard is true and ten times worse. My mother and her friends could have taught Generals Patton and MacArthur a thing or two. I couldn't take it anymore. I had to make a strategic retreat."

He grinned. "Any particular reason why you chose the hardware store as your haven?"

There were many reasons, but none she dared admit aloud. Opting for the one that would reveal the least, she volunteered, "My mom likes you. She's sure you'll back up anything she says. I'm afraid I led her to believe I'd listen to your advice."

"Ouch. I'm not sure if I'm ready for that kind of pressure."

"Don't worry. I don't want a thing from you. I can

just tell her you were waiting on a long line of customers and had no time for me."

He cast her a sideways glance. "I'd be all for that . . . except the store is empty. We'd be lying."

"Not exactly." She marched to the counter and stood at attention. "I am in line. And the store does have people in it. You and me."

"You and me," he echoed softly.

As if drawn to him like a magnet, Denise placed her elbows on the counter. "I won't tell if you won't."

Something flashed in his eyes for a split second before he stepped back, creating a larger gap between them. "It won't be true, anyway. We are about to have company. My sister Lindsay is due within the hour."

Lindsay's arrival sounded like an answer to a prayer. "That's terrific. I really need her help."

"I talked to her the other night about the theater and your plans for it. She's really excited."

"Do you really think so? She might change her mind when she sees that Payton really is just a small town."

"She's excited because it *is* a small town. That's been her dream, to be part of a small theater. She's really dying to become a part of a community and set down some roots."

"Payton does have that kind of feel to it."

"I agree. And if I know her, she's going to be chomping at the bit to make a good impression on you."

The idea that someone would go out of the way to impress her made Denise laugh. "Me?"

"Yes, you. You're the owner," he said with a wink. "Remember?"

She remembered, but she also recalled how at first she hadn't even wanted the gift, hadn't known what to do with it. She hadn't wanted to be responsible for so much. But now, all of a sudden, Denise couldn't wait for the opportunity to prove to herself that she could follow through on projects, that she could do something worthwhile.

As that thought sunk in, Denise looked at Ethan in surprise. "Oh my gosh. How did everything get so big? This theater has turned my life around and it's about to change other lives too."

"Change is not always a bad thing."

"I don't think so, either, but pulling it all off does worry me. What if Lindsay hates it?" she asked, voicing her fears. "What if our crazy ghost spooks off any prospective backers or ticket buyers?"

He played along. "What if I completely screw up the electricity and the whole thing either goes dark during Act III or sets off a spark and sets the building on fire?"

Just the thought of a fire made her nervous. "Don't say that!"

"Why not? You're obviously thinking about the worst case scenarios."

"Okay. From now on, I'm only going to think positively. But, let's not jinx a thing."

His green eyes flickered. "I won't do that," he said softly.

They stood across from each other, Denise feeling his presence more than ever.

Ethan tapped his finger on the counter. "You know, I was exaggerating a little when I said my sister was about to be here. She probably won't show up for another two hours."

"Oh."

"But, I'm hungry. You want to go down to The Grill and get a burger?"

"What about your store?"

"I'll put a sign on the door telling people I'll be back in an hour."

Denise couldn't help but smile at the notion that he would even consider doing such a thing. "Yet another difference between Payton and the big city."

"I'll take it. This is a particularly good difference." With a wink, he said, "So, how about lunch?"

Caution entered. Denise thought of Rachel, of Chad, of her mother and her matchmaking ways. She thought of the night before, when all she'd done was sit by herself and wish she wasn't alone.

Then, Denise met his gaze, and for the first time in a long time, she let her heart guide her. There was really only one answer she wanted to give to Ethan Flynn. "I'd love to have lunch with you," she said.

"Good."

Denise followed him out the door and then watched him write a quick note and place it on the frame with tape. "You know, suddenly, I think I'm hungry too."

"Good." He wrote a quick note and hung it on the frame with painter's tape. Then, he held out his hand.

Like an eager child at a fair, she took it and held on tight.

Chapter Twelve

The Grill was hopping. Almost every table was filled with people, eager to enjoy one of the last crisp fall days in Payton before the cool weather blew in.

Ethan had known from the first week of living in the small town that the bar and grill was exactly the place for him. The food was good, the atmosphere completely casual, and the service staff experienced.

He enjoyed sitting in the courtyard. He felt like he belonged, and he could also readily admit that he liked sitting there with Denise. Also clad in jeans and a t-shirt, she looked pretty and vibrant sitting across from him. Her casual attire had been accessorized with a pink scarf through her belt loops, some dangly pearl earrings, and her glorious hair was pulled back in some kind of metal clip.

She looked downright beautiful.

She was also very chatty. Over and over she shared funny anecdotes about her family, her previous job, and her chance meetings with movie stars in California.

Her stories, and her sense of irony about the most mundane tasks, kept him entertained through a double cheeseburger, two sodas, and a plate of chili-cheese fries.

He was just trying to figure out a way to convince her to have an ice cream cone with him when his sister wandered over.

"Lindsay!" he said, standing up. "When did you get in?"

"About twenty minutes ago, no thanks to you," she added, giving him a warm hug. "I can't believe you were able to just pop a sign on your store and go to lunch."

"People have to eat." Turning to Denise, he said, "This is Lindsay, my sister."

Lindsay straightened her shoulders. "Hi. I'm Lindsay Flynn."

"It's nice to meet you. I'm Denise Reece," she replied, before pointedly glancing at her watch. "Gosh, this lunch was far longer than I'd planned on," she said quickly. "I better get going and let you two visit. I'll just be on my way."

Not even a long lost sister was going to make Ethan cut his time with Denise short. Too rarely did just the two of them spend time together. "Please. Don't go yet."

She paused and caught his gaze.

Unable to help himself, he smiled, not even caring that his sister was witnessing his lovesick behavior.

"Well . . . all right."

Victory. "Have a seat. Linds, you hungry?"

"Yes." Lindsay sent a look his way that was a lot like the ones she used to give him when she wanted to join in his football games but knew he wouldn't let her—irritated but resolute.

Eager to get his sister settled, he said, "Here. Look at the menu. We just finished, but I was thinking some ice cream might hit the spot. Weren't you too, Denise?"

"I'm stuffed. But I'll stay while you eat, Lindsay." As she looked at their half-filled plate of fries, she said, "I don't know how you can eat another bite, Ethan."

Lindsay laughed. "I know why. It's a family thing. My mom was a horrible cook. We eat all our food whenever it's half-way decent."

"Great mom, no good in the kitchen," Ethan said between bites of French fries.

Denise chuckled. "At our house, it was just the opposite. My mom can cook really well, but with five kids you had to eat fast or everything would be all gone."

"From what I saw last time I was there, things haven't changed much," Ethan said.

"I'm just glad to meet you today," Lindsay said with a smile. "I have to admit I was pretty nervous about meeting you. I didn't think I'd sleep at all until our appointment tomorrow morning."

Denise couldn't help but be surprised at the statement. No one had ever acted worried or nervous around her before; she'd always been the girl in the background, overlooked or overshadowed by her siblings. In contrast, Lindsay seemed so outgoing, so completely at ease and full of confidence.

But, as Denise looked at her a little more closely, she could see some tell-tale signs of nervousness.

Lindsay's hands were clenched and nervously fiddling with a corner of the tablecloth. More than once, she darted a questioning look toward her brother.

She recognized the behavior. It was the same thing she would have done when she wanted to fit in but was unsure if she really could. One thing that had always helped calm her nerves was getting down to business, so she took out a pen and paper and spoke. "Obviously, I've never had a theater before. Do you have any thoughts on what direction it should take?"

Lindsay's shoulders visibly relaxed. "I do." Briefly, they discussed pros and cons of different operational plans, various types of community theaters, and finally, Lindsay's own experiences.

Lindsay's cheeseburger came while they talked, as did vanilla ice cream for Ethan. Denise sipped coffee as they continued their discussion.

Finally, Lindsay said, "Ethan said the theater's haunted. What's the story with that?"

Thankful that Lindsay acted more interested than mocking, Denise shared what she knew about Sally and

Flo's journals. She also relayed what had been happening with the construction workers' boom box, the talcum powder scent, and the windows mysteriously opening.

Lindsay listened raptly. "Do you think you'll be scared living there?"

"No. Quite honestly, I think the ghost really is Sally, and if anything, I think these actions are just meant to welcome me."

Ethan scoffed. "How can an open window be a sign?"

"Well, she is opening them, not locking them shut," Denise reasoned. "And the music has been nice. Strange, but nice."

Lindsay leaned forward, her expression animated. "I told Ethan that we ought to play up her presence. What do you think about our first play having something to do with ghosts?"

"I had the same idea."

"It's almost November now. If we have our first play around the beginning of December, the folks will already be in a holiday spirit. It should bring in people, no problem."

"December?" Denise exclaimed. "That seems so soon!"

"The work is going well," Ethan interjected.

"And I think we need to get something started while the momentum is still there," Lindsay said. "If we let the place get empty again, people might think there's something wrong with it."

"That does make sense."

"So is she hired?" Ethan asked, looking anxious to get up from the table now that they were all done eating.

Lindsay moaned. "Ethan!"

"Let's still keep our appointment," Denise said. "We can talk some more, then I've got to meet with my dad and brother and make sure I can hire you."

"They're lawyers," Ethan added.

"Aunt Flo left a lot of conditions in her will. If I don't follow them closely, it will mess up a lot of people's plans," Denise explained.

"That makes sense. I'll be with Ethan if you need anything," she said after they finalized the details surrounding their next appointment.

Denise stood up to leave. "Well, now I'll really let you two go. I'm sure you have a lot to catch up on."

"I'll walk you out," Ethan said.

After saying goodbye to Lindsay, Denise took Ethan's hand. "She's great, Ethan."

"She liked you," he said.

"I liked her. You were right. She seems perfect for our job."

He gave her hand a little squeeze. "So, I was thinking, why don't you come over soon? We could have dinner or something."

The thought of seeing Ethan, alone, delighted her. She teased, "Like, a date?"

"Precisely like a date."

The idea sounded great, but although her heart knew

she wanted to be near him, her brain was still sending out warning signals.

As if he read her mind, Ethan blurted, "Look. I don't know what's going to happen between us. Maybe we'll fall in love. Maybe we'll just be friends. Regardless, I'd like to see you again." He glanced at her sideways. "We'll just hang out. We don't have to do anything special. It will be fun."

It would. She'd love to sit next to him with nothing to do. Of course, she'd love to sit next to him and do a lot of things as well. "Okay."

He quirked an eyebrow. "That's it? Okay?"

"How about I come by on Tuesday night?"

"Deal. Jeff and I are planning to sand and stain the wood floors over the next few days." He sighed. "I really hate that job. This will give me something to look forward to. It's a date."

Quickly, Denise kissed his cheek, then went on her way, whistling under her breath as she walked to her car near the historical museum.

She had a date on Tuesday night!

No, it wasn't going to be an actual date. More just a hanging out session. Dates meant dresses and flirting.

This was going to be more along the lines of being good friends. Hanging out. Watching TV. Not a thing romantic about that.

But . . . there could be, she supposed, as she pictured Ethan at ease in his own home.

Other visions of him kept intruding, like Ethan picking up boxes from the theater's attic and moving them around like they were soft bean bags and then flexing his muscles and brushing back his hair under a ball cap.

Maybe he'd wear those favorite jeans of his, the ones that looked like they were so old and worn they'd feel like velvety-soft cotton.

She hoped so . . . not that it really mattered.

Because it *wasn't* going to be a date.

Chapter Thirteen

"I never liked repairing wood floors," Jeff mumbled Tuesday afternoon as he measured another plank and made yet another mark on the floor. "This old wood doesn't want to be bent, nailed, or conformed to any other piece." He hammered in another finishing nail, then winced. "And this wood is giving me splinters. They're hurting like the devil."

"I've had my share too," Ethan admitted, knowing that even with a handful of splinters he still wouldn't break down and slip on a pair of gloves. He enjoyed feeling the grain under his fingertips too much. "At least your wife will help you get them out."

"Injuries do have their rewards," Jeff joked. "In a few hours, it will all be worth it. Things are looking real good."

Ethan looked up from the miter box where he was fitting a new piece and had to agree. While the major repairs had gone quickly enough, the finishing was a real bear.

And to top it off, he'd had some inventory problems over at the store. For two weeks, a shipment had been delayed, stuck on some train car that had derailed. Now he had about forty boxes in his back room, begging to be inventoried and displayed. Allen, and his two college-aged employees had their hands full too. Everyone in town was coming in, needing materials for their fall projects.

"We're almost done," he said. "We should be able to sand and stain within two hours."

"I'll put on the polyurethane coats after that." In direct contrast to his earlier comment, Jeff ran a hand over the planks. "This sure is a beauty, though. Something about the workmanship sixty years ago that does a heart good."

"Amen to that," Ethan said. He'd already had a notebook full of architectural designs that he'd sketched from various points in the old building. They would come in handy in his next architectural class.

They worked in silence for the next hour, their only conversation being measurements and instructions. Neither minded; Ethan enjoyed the quiet, it gave him time to think about the woman about to be living two floors above him. Something was happening between them, and he was afraid it had far more to do with inner feelings than mere attraction.

Ethan sanded the plank in his hands, rubbing the grain until it flowed like satin under his hands. It wasn't until Jeff was standing right next to him that he even noticed him. "What's up?"

"I'm done for now. I think we better go ahead and wait to stain tomorrow, when the light's better."

More time had passed than he'd realized. "Okay. See you tomorrow."

As Jeff put his tools away and then opened the door, whistling under his breath, Ethan sat back on his heels and tried to only think about work. But, all that kept coming to mind was Denise's smile and the soft brush of her lips against his cheek.

Finally, he gave up and went home. There, he greeted Comet, his golden Lab, took him for a quick run, and then grabbed a tall glass of iced tea. Finally he and Comet went out to his screen porch and sat down. Although the late October air was chilly, the sun was out and the air smelled crisp and clean. He'd just read through eight pages of assigned reading when his doorbell rang.

Denise had arrived, as promised. "Hey," he said.

"Hi," she said hesitantly. "Are you busy?"

"Not at all. I was just sitting out back, catching up on reading. Want to come on back?"

"Sure."

As they passed through the kitchen, he poured her an ice tea. Finally, when they were seated across from each other, Denise presented him with a tentative smile.

"I was just by the theater and saw the wood floors. They're beautiful."

"Thanks. Jeff and I think so too."

"Tomorrow you'll stain?"

"That's the plan." He winced as he stretched his fingers. Denise frowned.

"What's wrong?"

"Nothing. The old wood isn't very forgiving. It fought back when I tried to make it behave," he said, showing off his right hand, complete with a good six splinters. The skin around each was red and puffy.

She touched each mark carefully. "These look like they hurt."

She was acting like he'd sustained major injuries. It was actually kind of nice. "They're no big deal, though they do hurt," he added, thankful Jeff wasn't around to hear him.

She glanced at him sharply, her eyes narrowing.

"I'll be fine."

"Maybe. Maybe not. I do know you ought to take them out, though."

"You sound like an expert. Ever gotten a mess of splinters in your right hand?"

She jutted up her chin. "As a matter of fact, I have."

"What did you do?"

"I asked someone to take them out for me." She brightened. "Want to call Stratton?"

"No way am I going to call a doctor for this. I'll deal with my hand later."

"You won't." Standing up, she asked, "Do you have a first aid kit or something?"

"I do. It's under the kitchen sink."

Within minutes, Denise was back, a pleasant smile hovering as she brought over a towel.

"I went ahead and put this in some warm water. Give me your hand."

He gave it willingly, noticing how gentle she was as she rubbed the towel over his thumb, fingers, and palm. "Oh, Ethan. I'm so sorry you got so hurt repairing my theater."

He'd gotten a splinter, not a dislocated shoulder, but, in a purely masculine way, he knew there was no problem with milking it a little. "I'll be okay as soon as these are out," he said.

"Your skin is all red."

"They do hurt," he murmured.

She rubbed his hand again, massaging the fleshy part of his palm. It was all he could do not to moan. Her slim, cool fingers felt perfect against his own.

She probably had no idea how much he liked her touch. Or, did she? Her gaze was as warm as her hands.

"Ethan, I think the best way would be just to use a needle and tweezers and tackle each one, right after the other. Are you okay with that?"

"Sure."

She leaned forward, bringing with her the soft scent of her hair, and the further softness of her curves. Ethan did his best to concentrate on the needles.

Quickly, she went to work, tackling each angry splinter with precision.

Ethan hardly felt any pain, he was too intent on watching her bite her bottom lip and feeling her soft fingers caress his hand.

"Three down, three to go. Are you doing okay? Would you like a break?"

He wanted a great many things. The top of his list involved holding her in his arms and kissing her senseless. "I think I can handle it."

Her gray eyes turned liquid. "I hope I'm not hurting you too much."

"You've got gentle hands, Dee."

"Thanks." She bent over his palm again, pricking the skin, then patiently coaxing the splinter of wood out. "Got it!" she said.

He'd hardly felt it. Perversely, he found himself wishing he had a whole lot more wrong with him. It had been quite a while since he'd been so aware of a woman.

Rachel had never affected him this way, which was probably why he'd never been terribly heartbroken when they'd ended the relationship. "I'm so glad you're here to do this," he murmured.

"Me too. Ethan, what do you think you would have done if I hadn't stopped by?"

She sounded exactly like a prim schoolteacher, all starch and polish. Yet, now he spied a sparkle in her eyes, like she knew exactly that he wasn't all that hurt but was just playing along.

"I guess I would have just suffered through."

Her lips twitched. "Gosh, I just might have to check on you tomorrow too."

He could hardly wait. Trying to look doubtful, he said, "Think you can spare the time?"

"I will, if you need me too," she said, laughing.

Ethan bit his lip to keep from grinning.

Quickly, she pressed her lips to one of the many red marks on his hand. "It's the least I could do."

Her lips felt like heaven. "I'll plan on it, then."

Next, she bathed his hand in antiseptic wash, then massaged ointment into his skin.

He knew he'd be washing the goo off the moment she left.

But for now, there was no reason but to enjoy every single bit of medicinal attention he could. "Mmm," he said.

"Does that feel good?"

"Very good. Thanks so much, Denise."

She smiled. "I'm glad I came over."

"Me, too. I was looking forward to having you here."

Ethan glanced at her more closely, enjoying the way the breeze filtered through his screen door and fluffed the hair around her face. She looked young and fresh.

At ease.

And now that he was out of his splinter induced fog, he saw that for once, she looked peaceful, serene.

"I know I promised you dinner, but how about we just

order a pizza and play a board game. Ever played Scrabble?"

Challenge entered her expression. "Once or twice."

"How about a game?"

"You sure? I mean, I'd hate to trounce you when you're so injured and all."

"I think you're just afraid that I'm going to shame you mercilessly."

"Shame me? I didn't know hardware guys were so good at spelling."

He played dumb. "What? You have to be able to spell in Scrabble?"

She laughed. "You're on."

"Good. Let's go on inside. Now that the sun is going down, the temperature's dropped. I'll order the pizza and make us some coffee."

She followed him obediently, a hint of a smile running across her lips as she patted Comet, who trotted in along with them.

Her smile made him recall just how sweet it had been to hold her in his arms. "Dee, come here."

And then she was in his arms, kissing him back.

After several heated minutes, he pulled away. "Coffee," he said.

"Scrabble," she replied.

He pointed to the table. She sat.

They were both too breathless to say a word.

Chapter Fourteen

"**I**'m calling it a night," Jeff said from the doorway of Denise's new apartment two weeks later. "It's eight o'clock and I can hardly move."

"Thanks so much for your help," Denise said, leaning her head against the back of the couch. "Thanks for everything."

"No problem," he called out, right before he walked down the steps to the first floor. His footsteps echoed, as did his whistling as he opened and shut the theater's heavy front door securely behind him. The sound of it connecting reverberated through the empty building.

"I'll need to go down and lock that soon," Denise said from her spot next to Ethan on the couch. "That is, if I can ever move again."

Ethan groaned. "Don't mention moving."

She laughed as she looked around. The couch was surrounded by boxes, fake plants, too many books, and a pungent smell of fresh paint. Every muscle was sore, and she was exhausted from carrying so much up three flights of stairs. "I may just sit here all night," she said. "This is the only clean place in the whole building."

Ethan picked up an old t-shirt of her brother's from the couch and wrinkled his nose as he got a good whiff of it. "I hate to tell you this . . . but it's not that clean."

She giggled. "You're right. Maybe Sally will take pity on me and do some midnight cleaning. I don't think my muscles can lift one more thing."

He flexed his right arm. "I feel the same way. I don't know how we even got this couch upstairs. I thought it was going to fall on my head about three different times."

"It's good you're so strong," she said, loving their silly conversation. "And, it's good so many people helped us out."

"We've got a good group of family and friends."

She knew he was right. Her family had spent hours helping her unpack her storage unit, her car, and her room at her parents. In addition, it had been Kevin who had given her his old living room furniture, even though she could tell his wife was having a hard time giving away perfectly good things.

They had all climbed the three flights of stairs numerous times, bringing sandwiches, drinks, and chips with them. Dinah brought over a bunch of cookies, and Lindsay had even unpacked most of her kitchen.

Thinking of that, Denise said, "Well, at least I'll be able to brew coffee in the morning."

"That sounds pretty good about now." He sat up. "Do you have any decaf?"

"I think so. Well, somewhere."

"I'll go make us some."

"You don't mind?" Denise asked, grateful for his offer but not wanting to take advantage of him. "If you want to leave, I perfectly understand."

"What? When we're alone at last?"

His quip caught her off guard and made her feel warm inside. Though they'd spent a lot of time together during the last few weeks, working on her apartment and the plans for the theater, Denise had felt as if they'd been tiptoeing over the thing that was at the top of her mind: their kiss.

Quickly she glanced at him, though she couldn't meet his gaze since he was rummaging around in her kitchen.

As if he sensed her attention, Ethan said, "I've thought a lot about the other night."

She knew exactly what night he was talking about. "Me too."

After a few minutes, he returned, along with the aromatic scent of fresh coffee brewing. "It should be ready in a few minutes."

"All right." Warily, she watched him sit back next to

her, though the feeling in the room had changed. It was now more charged. Electric.

Her attention switched from sore muscles to his scent, his proximity to her, and to their relationship, and to what kind of relationship they had.

As if he read her mind, he said, "I guess one day we're going to have to explore what's between us."

"I guess so."

"So . . . you think you'll be ready for another relationship any time soon?"

"Probably." Oh, who was she kidding? She'd just spent the last two weeks remembering how it felt to be in his arms, daydreaming about kissing him on this very couch! "Definitely."

"That's good." He eyed her. "Um, I hope you don't think that I led Rachel on. I never meant to."

His explanation was touching, but unnecessary. "I know you didn't. Believe me, she and I see the world very differently."

He nodded. "I've dated a lot but was never really serious before her. And to tell you the truth, she was just someone easy to be with. Our relationship just . . . happened."

"I believe it." She was just about to expand on that, when she heard a soft scratching downstairs. "Did you hear that?"

"What?"

"Listen." After a few heartbeats, they heard a soft scratching again.

Chills raised the hairs on her arms. Her pulse quickened. "What do you think that is?" she whispered.

"No telling. Maybe a cat?"

A cat. *Of course.* A cat sounded completely reasonable. "I never did go downstairs to check everything after Jeff left, to make sure the place was locked up," she murmured. "I bet there's a door open or something."

"I bet you're right." He stood up. "Do you want to stay here while I go look around?"

Something rattled again, making her stomach knot.

While it was tempting to let him take care of everything, it wasn't her way . . . and it wasn't the way she wanted to be with him. "No. I want to come too. Unless you think whatever made that noise has left the building?"

He tilted his head. "Kind of like Elvis? No. If it's a cat, it's probably going to wander until we let it out. Come on." He held out a hand.

She took it gratefully.

Slowly, they walked toward her door, then descended the stairs. Dim lights guided their way, though the stark contrast between her carpeted apartment and the vacuous theater was striking.

Where she had small spaces and coziness, the theater was wide open, dusty, and huge. The wooden stairs echoed with each step they took.

Soon, they were on the second floor landing. "Do you see anything?" she asked Ethan, who was two steps ahead of her.

"Nope. Here, kitty, kitty," he called out, his voice teasing.

Standing still, Denise strained to hear a little 'meow' reply, a chuckle, Jeff saying he forgot a power tool, or anything that would be easily explained.

But all they heard was silence.

"Let's go down and make sure the front door and all those windows are securely shut."

"I'll follow," she said, unable to hide her trepidation.

Slowly, they descended again. Her eyes scanned the open room, with the theater seats on their left and the large, ornate foyer to the right.

As if on cue, a cool breeze greeted them on the second step. "Ah, there we go," Ethan said. "That window's open again."

She should have felt relief, but didn't. The last time they'd found a window open, she'd shrugged it off as negligence, but this time, it felt like too much of a coincidence. Maybe it was the ghost.

Or what if there was someone in the theater? A burglar? Quickly, Denise clutched his hand and held on tight.

He squeezed it in response. "We'll be okay."

Slowly, they walked through the empty rooms, finding nothing other than the faint scent of talcum powder and a stack of papers on the floor.

Sally had visited them again. Denise was sure of it.

Not that she was going to tell Ethan that.

But then Ethan stumbled. "I could have sworn this

was put away," he said, picking up his tool belt and placing it on an old table.

"Maybe one of the guys threw it on the ground?"

Ethan looked doubtful but said nothing.

"Well, I guess everything's fine after all."

"You sure?"

"I'm sure. I'm probably just tired. And if we do have a ghost, I don't think she means any harm."

"I hope not," he said, stepping closer.

She gasped as she felt his body next to hers.

"Relax," he said with a slight smile. "I don't mean you any harm, either."

His smile was anything but innocent. "For some reason, I trust you less than a sixty-year-old ghost."

"Why is that?" he asked.

"Maybe because of the way you make me feel."

"Which is?"

Did she dare say it? "Off-kilter. Like I'm not sure what to do."

"I feel the same way around you."

"Really?"

"Absolutely, Denise. Believe me, you were not in my plans."

"You weren't in mine, either," she said, her voice curiously husky. "I think I'm falling for you. You make me feel happy, alive." She shook her head. "All I wanted when I came back to Payton was to straighten everything out with the theater, and possibly become closer to my family. I never imagined I'd head right into another relationship."

"What we have feels right," Ethan whispered.

A steadying sense of peace coursed through her. "That's it exactly." As he circled his arms around her, guiding her closer, she murmured, "So, what do you think—"

"Kiss me."

Before she could question him on the logic of that idea, his lips found hers, and she found heaven in his arms.

Just for a moment. Just before they heard another crash.

Chapter Fifteen

"Well, look at that," Joanne said. "Who would have thought?"

"Not me. I had it on good authority that my brother was completely done with relationships," Lindsay quipped.

Denise felt her cheeks heat, just like a teenager. "Is there a reason you two are in my theater, uninvited?"

"Listen to you! Just an hour ago, when I was lugging your clothes upstairs, you didn't want me to leave," Joanne quipped. "Back then, you enjoyed my company."

"I did appreciate your help. And I did enjoy your company . . . but not right now."

"We're busy," Ethan said, giving his sister an evil eye. "Come back tomorrow."

Joanne looked incredulous. "No way. It's you who

needs to head out, Ethan. Lindsay and I brought snacks and ice cream. We're going to have a slumber party."

He turned to Denise, surprised. "You had a slumber party planned?"

"No." She darted a glance toward Lindsay and Denise. They both looked amused, and not the slightest bit embarrassed for interrupting the two of them.

Joanne shook her sack of ice cream. "Unplanned things are the best. Come on. This will be fun. You don't want to spend your first night here alone, with just Sally, do you?"

"I'd be careful about how you say that," Ethan said. "She's probably awake and busily haunting as we speak."

Both women looked surprised. "Is that why you two are making out in the foyer?" Joanne asked.

"That's what I'd be doing," Lindsay quipped.

"We were not making out . . . merely getting acquainted," Ethan corrected.

Denise nodded.

Joanne lifted an eyebrow. "Acquainted."

"We heard a noise," Denise said, trying again. "The window popped open again."

Lindsay walked over and shut the window securely. "Well, that's taken care of." She held up a canvas tote bag. "Guess what? We brought books! We can research our ghost as we eat."

That did sound pretty good. Spending more time in Ethan's arms sounded dangerous. Nothing else seemed to matter when she was kissing him. "Okay."

Ethan frowned. "I guess I'll go ahead and leave. Call me if you need anything," he murmured, squeezing her hand.

"Gosh, and you made coffee. I'm sorry . . ."

His gaze gentled. "It's okay. It's probably for the best, anyway. What's happening between us, it's happening fast . . . almost too fast. See you tomorrow."

As soon as he left, Denise was escorted by the two women back upstairs. When all the doors were securely locked, coffee poured, and snacks pulled out, Joanne leaned forward.

"So, what's the story?"

"With Ethan? I don't know. It's nothing serious."

"It looked like it was."

Actually, it had felt that way too. "It could be, if we were in different places."

"You mean like not living above a haunted theater?" Lindsay asked.

"I mean like not just getting over hurt feelings," Denise explained. "I can't pretend that I'm ready to fall head over heels again. I'm not."

"I understand."

"And, this family," Denise added. "Even if I had everything under control with Ethan, I'd have to worry about everyone else. Everyone is commenting on us. It's enough to drive a girl crazy!"

"I bet," Lindsay said.

"Even when I think I'm going to be alone, I'm not."

Joanne blinked, but not before Denise spied a hurt look. "Like tonight?" Joanne asked.

Now she'd made things worse. "Please don't take this the wrong way. It's just that I have a lot to sort through, but no time to do it. I got used to being alone in California."

"Denise, we're sisters. We've shared a thousand late nights, from the times we sneaked into the kitchen for ice cream to covering for each other in high school during curfews. Have you forgotten?"

"Of course not."

Joanne shook her head. "Sometimes, it seems that you have. You moved away. You didn't even call me when Chad broke your heart. You've pretended that the four of us weren't there for you when we were growing up, but we were."

"I know."

"You know? Then how about not making us all work so hard?" Joanne said, impatience peppering her words. "We like you! And somewhere in that hard, stubborn head of yours, I know that you like us too. I'm not going to let you compartmentalize your family."

Joanne leaned forward. "Like Cam and I said the other day, we know this crazy, too-big, too-loud family can be overwhelming and intrusive. But I also know, for a fact, that we're really lucky to have each other. I've accomplished many things because I've known I've had my family's support. So have Cameron, Kevin, and Jeremy."

Propping a hand on her hip, Joanne glared at Denise. "Space and independence aren't all they're cracked up to be. Sitting on the couch with just a book or television for company gets old fast."

Denise knew that too. She was just about to say so when Joanne continued.

"And marriage is terrific, but it's even more special when you share your feelings with the people who were with you before it all happened, and will be when it's all over. I'll always be your sister, Denise. I'll always be there for you. I'll always want to be a part of your life." She sighed. "When are you going to be ready to make that pledge to me? Because, if you want to know the truth, I could sure use a sister these days. I've missed having one."

Just when Denise opened her mouth to reassure her that she felt the same way, Joanne—and her famous temper—ran into the bathroom.

Denise glanced at Lindsay helplessly.

"It's going to be okay," Lindsay said. "I promise. Come on, let's fix some popcorn."

Denise did as she suggested, and before long, Joanne came out and hugged Denise.

Then, the three of them got out the books, opened them up to earmarked pages, switched from decaf to hot chocolate, and gabbed just like Denise and Joanne used to do.

They got out old photo albums and laughed over the Reece siblings, discussed Ethan and the future of the theater, and finally drifted off to sleep. As she closed her eyes, Denise had to admit that her sister had been right. She did have a closet full of memories with her family, and they were just as important as love and any other future plans.

As she finally slept, Denise wondered why it had taken her so long to remember that.

Chapter Sixteen

"How come some people have all the luck?" Lindsay asked Denise as they walked along Payton's scenic bike trail.

The comment struck Denise as funny, though most of what Lindsay said struck her that way. Lindsay Flynn was one of the most charismatic, free spirited people she knew. "What do you mean?"

Lindsay smiled at her quip. "In the 'Lifestyle' section of the *Payton Registrar*, there was an article about how Payton and Priscilla Chase just won an award for 'outstanding cuisine' or something like that. It seems like quite an achievement. Now, they're probably going to be featured on the Food Network." She shrugged. "I was just thinking publicity like that is hard to come by."

"I don't think luck had anything to do with it.

Priscilla is really talented. She won a bunch of awards in culinary school. She was a chef in a bistro in Houston before she moved here."

"I wonder why she moved to Payton."

"It's a long story. Let me just say that from what I heard, it wasn't an easy transition."

"I bet not. This town is a far cry from the big city."

"It is that. Of course, I heard from Jeremy that Priscilla was charmed by Payton Chase, the manager of the country club. That's why she ended up staying." Denise picked up a pinecone that had fallen in her path. "These are pretty."

"I love November," Lindsay agreed. "You ought to put some of those in a basket."

"Maybe." Denise put the cone in her backpack. "In any case, the club is lucky to have Priscilla Chase. Her reputation has highlighted the golf club, and our town, quite a bit. People are even beginning to appreciate her gourmet entrees, even though there's plenty who would prefer to only have prime rib and burgers served there."

Lindsay laughed. "I'll have to meet Priscilla. I'm finding myself strangely at home in this town, as well."

"You better be. I need your help with the theater."

Lindsay glanced at her, her expression changing from joking to far more serious in an instant. "Are you sure that you're okay with everything I've doing as theater manager? I kind of feel like I'm stealing your baby or something."

" 'Adopting' would be a better term," Denise corrected. Honestly, Lindsay, I have no desire to attempt to run a theater by myself, and even less of one to mess it up. My reputation is already in shreds; the last thing I need or want is for people to whisper that I'm a theater wrecker too."

"I've heard nothing but good things about Denise Reece."

"That's because you're new. Wait until the local gossip queens get hold of you."

Lindsay stretched her arms above her head as they paused at a corner. "All I know is that people are nice here. Even though I've never lived in a town this size, I knew almost from the very first that I fitted in here."

"It probably has something to do with Ethan. I've noticed that he's made a lot of friends."

"Ethan is friendly," Lindsay agreed. "It's his nature."

Denise couldn't help but think he was a lot of other things too.

"Earth to Denise," Lindsay said with a little clap. "Are you still with us?"

"Sorry. I guess my mind drifted off."

"Right toward my big brother, I bet."

"Maybe."

Lindsay's tentative smile turned all out. "*Maybe*? You have 'I-like-Ethan-Edward-Flynn' written all over you!"

Denise thought she probably did, since that was where her mind always wandered. "Ethan Edward?

Wow, your mom sure liked E's," she said, hoping to change the subject.

Lindsay didn't look fooled for a moment, but she didn't press either, so Denise felt grateful.

They walked along some more, Lindsay swinging her hands as they did so. The fall air was crisp, and more than a few cardinals flew by, their bright red feathers heralding the passing of autumn.

A couple of acquaintances passed; Denise said hello and introduced Lindsay to each.

Invigorated by the walk and the beauty of the bike trail, Denise felt some of her stress fade away. Sure, her life was kind of crazy, but it was also filled with a lot of good things. "You're going to love it here," Denise said to Lindsay as they approached the parking lot. "Have you thought about where you want to live?"

"Not yet. Right now I'm okay with Ethan and Comet. I'll look for a place once we get the first production behind us."

Turning her mind back to business, Denise said, "I think construction will be done at the end of the month. When do you think we can begin considering a specific play to put on?"

"I have an idea." Lindsay slowed her steps as she turned to Denise. "You know how we talked about highlighting the rumors about the theater being haunted?"

It *was* haunted. There was no doubt in Denise's mind. "I remember."

"What do you think about *Scrooge* being our first play? There's all kinds of ghosts in it, and it's a familiar show for most people. Plus, I directed it in college, so I already know the script and what works."

"I think *Scrooge* will be a great initial production. But, it's already the second week in November. Do you think producing a play in six weeks will be pushing things too quickly?"

"My gut feeling is that it would be best to push things. That way people are motivated and we'll get some immediate backers."

Denise couldn't help but feel that things were moving along at warp speed. Everything was coming together so quickly, she felt like she could hardly hang on. "I think that's a fine idea."

"You sure? You sound kind of hesitant."

"I was just thinking that everything is happening so fast. I'm hoping that we're making the right decisions."

"This theater is going to be successful. I can feel it. And, if you're worrying about Ethan, I think that's going to work out just fine too. I know he likes you, Denise."

"He just got over a relationship."

"You mean that whole thing with Rachel? I don't know how involved he really was."

"I think she thought it was pretty involved."

"That girl's delusional. She thinks choosing the correct wallpaper is pretty intense."

"My mother would too."

"So . . ."

Did she really want to discuss this with Ethan's sister?

"Ethan and I . . . like each other," Denise said, struggling to find the best words to express her feelings. "But, we've also got a lot of baggage. I was in a serious relationship before I moved here. He just finished with Rachel."

"We've already gone through this."

"You're right . . . but there's other things too. I'm just now rebuilding relationships with my family. Over the years I think I kind of forgot what was important." She sighed. "Then, there's the whole theater thing."

"It's haunted and going to be beautiful."

"Since it was left to me, I feel like I need to take care of it . . ."

"You're doing that," Lindsay interrupted.

"I suppose. It's just that right now, I feel that I need to take things one step at a time. Take things slow."

"I've never had time to fall in love. But if I was that kind of person, I think I'd grab hold of the opportunity with both hands."

"You make me laugh. No one *plans* on falling in love. It just happens."

"Not to me, it doesn't," Lindsay retorted. "I've got my life perfectly planned out. I'm going to work until my mid-thirties, then find someone suitable, and then settle down and have children."

"Your 2.5 children?"

"Maybe."

Denise chuckled. "It's now my turn to give you a piece of advice. Nothing ever turns out the way you plan. Life's full of surprises."

Lindsay stared at her hard, then chuckled as well. "Sounds as if you need to start listening to yourself, Denise."

Chapter Seventeen

The theater was dark except for a lone candle flickering on the stage. The smell of sawdust, paint, and brass polish filled the air, along with a sense of foreboding and confusion.

Ethan propped a foot on his opposite knee and wondered how in the world he ended up sitting in an empty theater at eight o'clock that night.

Except, it wasn't too empty. He was with Denise, Joanne, and Stratton. They were having a makeshift séance.

Ethan hoped no one from his hometown would ever hear he had ever been a part of such a thing.

Which made him ask once again, "Denise, are you sure this is what you want to be doing tonight?"

She looked at him like he was crazy. "Of course. I just got this book in from the library," she said, holding up a tattered hardcover with a picture of a murky lake and broken-down rowboat. "It's all about getting to know ghosts."

It was all he could do to keep a straight face.

As he glanced at Joanne and Stratton, he wondered how the Reece family ever got through life. Each family member seemed to throw himself or herself wholeheartedly into a project, not even caring how silly it was. Didn't they ever just say 'no'?

Take what they were doing, for instance. Sitting in the newly painted auditorium of the theater, watching Denise, and attempting to formulate a plan to meet the magical ghost face-to-face. It sounded like some junior high sleepover, only without the talk about girls or the infamous ouija board.

Of course, most guys he knew just didn't get into this stuff.

Joanne and Denise were now hunched over a book and reading it, Joanne taking copious notes. It looked like they were going to be there for quite a while.

Carefully, he eyed Stratton. The town's doctor looked as ready to sit and wait for elusive ghosts as the rest of them. Ethan leaned over and finally asked his burning question to the only seemingly sane person around. "Why, exactly, did we encourage this?"

Stratton raised an eyebrow, looked both ways to make sure the coast was clear, then spoke. "Several reasons. One, because our girls want us to be here. Two, it beats another night sitting in front of the TV. Three, if Joanne gets scared, she's going to run into my arms." He said the last with the kind of smile that guys perfected when they were juniors in high school.

Ethan could appreciate both the smile and the idea behind it. But just to clarify, he said, "So, you don't believe in the ghost?"

Stratton shrugged. "I don't know what to believe. I've seen some pretty crazy things in medicine. People have become critically ill and remarkably better in a day's time. Prayer has worked wonders. Fevers have come on, then vanished quicker than I would have ever guessed." He paused. "Actually, I've seen weirder things than haunted mansions."

The phrase made Ethan think of Disney Land, and the ride with the transparent ghosts. "I guess you're right," he said.

"I know I am. Besides, look at Dee and Jo. They're having a great time. Joanne has really missed her sister. This is giving them something to do."

Ethan leaned back in his chair and decided he had to agree. The sisters were sitting together, shoulders touching, and practically glowing from their contact with each other.

Just knowing how lonely Denise had been during her two years in California made him take Stratton's advice. There were other, just as important reasons for sitting in the theater.

As if Joanne instinctively knew he'd just come to that conclusion, she broke the silence.

"We've got a plan," Joanne announced, as if there were a hundred people inside of the auditorium instead of just the four of them. "We're going to talk to Sally, and talk to her about her scrapbook."

Stratton sipped his drink. "Honey, how will we know if she's here?"

"We'll know."

"In the past, she's opened windows, or you'll smell her," Denise chimed in.

Ethan said, "I've seen the open windows, but I haven't smelled a thing."

"What kind of smell are we talking here?" Stratton asked.

"Talcum powder," Denise replied.

"Anything else, Jo?" Stratton asked, looking as serious as could be.

Ethan shook his head. That man had one thing on his mind—Joanne in his arms.

Joanne nodded. "I think we need to tell her what Denise and I found out about how that snake, Ronald Morgan, made up that story about her so he could go to Hollywood. We found some old letters of his on the Internet," she explained to Stratton and Ethan.

Ethan figured if Sally could wander around the theater and turn on radios, she could probably figure out the rest of it. "Don't you think Sally might already know?"

Denise looked at him as if he'd sprouted wings. "Ethan, she's been haunting a theater. Do you really think she's had time to get on the Internet too?"

"No, I guess not. I guess haunting would probably be a full-time job."

"Exactly." After organizing all of them on a blanket spread out on the stage, Denise motioned for quiet. She opened her book and then started reading from the script. "Sally, please visit us," she said, her voice a little louder. "We have important news for you."

The four of them stared up at the ceiling. Ethan couldn't help feel a little chilled as every creak and groan from the theater took on new meaning.

Denise looked particularly agitated. "Sally?" she called out. "Are you here?"

The building creaked and groaned again. The candle in the middle of their makeshift circle flickered.

Stratton grunted as Joanne practically climbed on his lap.

Lucky dog.

Another creak echoed through the room. They all held their breaths.

Nothing happened. No ghostly appearances. No music from the boom box. Against his better judgment, Ethan sniffed the air.

Nope, no talcum powder scent, either.

Denise leaned forward. Looking earnest, she began to flip through the printed sheets she'd retrieved from the Internet. "See, Sally, it says here in this Chicago paper that Ronald was later found guilty of siphoning gasoline. And the girlfriend he left you for dumped him like a hot potato."

She pointed to another page. "Here is a quote from two of your co-actors in *Romeo and Juliet*. They said you were one of the most honest and good people they knew." She read further. "Oh! Here is an article about how they found Ronald with all the money he claimed you stole! They cleared your reputation!"

"That's cool," Joanne murmured from Stratton's arms.

Ethan couldn't help but be impressed as well. Denise had done a lot of work to ensure that a stranger from the past was going to have her name cleared. And, whether he was imagining it or not, something felt different in the room. It was as if the air felt thicker. Quickly, Ethan glanced at Stratton and Joanne to see if they were noticing anything, too.

They were sitting motionless, their focus completely on Denise. She kept talking. Over and over again, Denise retold the facts about Sally, what she had found out, how she was impressed with Sally's reputation, and how her great aunt had felt the same way.

The candle flickered again.

Finally, her voice slowed down, then drifted to a hoarse whisper. Ethan's heart went out to her. He knew she was disappointed by the lack of a response.

But honestly, what had she expected? A ghostly vision to pop out of the closet and thank her? An eerie voice to call out from the attic, commending her for everything she'd done?

He took a deep breath. If Denise wasn't careful, she was going to burst into tears. He knew her frustration stemmed from more than a wayward ghost. He knew she was still feeling the effects of moving, of her break-up with Chad, and of the pressure to refurbish the theater.

Ethan was just about to get up and go to her when she suddenly straightened and gasped. Joanne did too.

Even Stratton stilled.

Slowly, Ethan turned his head to where they were gazing. A window had just popped open. And if he didn't know better, a faint scent of talcum powder was tickling his nose.

Joanne popped up out of Stratton's lap. "Sally?" she called out, reaching for Denise's hand. "I believe in you. You're going to love this theater."

As the cool night's breeze flew in through the window, shocking them all with its burst of frost, Ethan had to admit that something pretty crazy was going on. Somewhere, somehow, there was another being in the room. He knew it as clearly as he knew when he had to make another order of lawn and garden equipment for his store.

Denise edged closer to him and grabbed his arm. He took advantage and pulled her toward him. She spoke. "Sally, I don't care if you stay here . . . but if you want to leave, I'll understand."

As her words echoed through the theater, an ominous creak emitted from the back stairway. Joanne gripped Stratton's shoulders. Ethan wrapped an arm around Denise.

She glanced at him gratefully. He sniffed again. He could smell nothing but dust and fresh paint.

But then, just as his head was about to tell himself that he was playing tricks on himself again, the boom box clicked on.

Denise and Joanne screamed.

Stratton grunted.

Ethan could admit it; he was ready to get the heck out of the place.

As an old Tommy Dorsey tune played, and as the chilly wind sent shivers down his spine, the door opened.

Joanne squealed again.

Denise grabbed his hand in a death grip.

And Lindsay walked in, carrying a pizza.

"Whoa," she said, glancing at their tense expressions. "Am I interrupting something?"

Her joviality was like a slap in the face, bringing all four of them out of their trance. Spurred by embarrassment that his sister caught him practically scared to death, he hastily stood up and turned to her. "What are you doing here?"

She stepped back. "I thought Denise might want some pizza. But I can go."

"No, stay," Denise said, a warm smile easing the tension. Standing up also, she walked toward his sister. "Sorry for the scene. We were just trying to contact Sally. The ghost."

Lindsay's eyebrows launched skyward. Ethan hoped she wasn't about to let out a sarcastic quip and embarrass Denise. She'd been through enough.

Thinking quickly, he said, "Actually, we—"

"Did see signs of her!" Joanne interjected. "It was like the scariest thing that's ever happened to me."

Stratton nodded. "It was pretty intense."

Lindsay placed the box on the floor. "No way."

"Oh, yeah." Joanne said, in no hurry to leave Stratton's lap. "Right before you came, the window popped open and the boom box clicked on."

"Oh my gosh!"

Stratton grinned. "It was pretty weird. I even smelled the powder."

Ethan glanced at them all in surprise. "I did too. I thought I was the only one."

Denise was glowing in triumph. "I'm so excited. I think she likes us. What do you think, Joanne?"

"I think if she wanted to scare us, she was doing a pretty good job," Joanne said.

"I wasn't terrified, more 'on edge,'" Denise admitted.

"You all looked pretty freaked out when I walked in the door," Lindsay said. "Ethan, you're one of the most logical people I know. What do you think about all this?"

It was on the tip of his tongue to name off about a

hundred reasons for a window popping open and a radio suddenly turning on. Faulty wiring, warped panes or mountings. Timers.

Someone could be pulling a prank on them.

But at the moment, none of those reasons seemed right or worthwhile to explain. After all, there really were benefits to having a scared girlfriend, he mused, as Denise slipped her arm around his waist.

"I did smell powder," he said.

They all waited for him to say more, to say what he really thought.

Denise, with her crystal clear gray eyes, gazed at him with hope.

Stratton grinned that trademark grin, Joanne watched him like he was the nightly news, and Lindsay tapped her foot, as impatient as ever.

Ethan swallowed hard. "I think Sally was here," he said.

Everyone stared at him in surprise, but no one said a word. Then, finally, the boom box started playing "In the Mood".

"How about some pizza?" Lindsay asked, clearing her throat. "It's an extra large from the Pizza Shack."

"I'd love some," Joanne said, "Being scared to death always gives me an appetite."

"Me too," said Denise. "Let's go upstairs and eat. I think I have some sodas."

As they all tromped up Denise's private stairs, Ethan

paused. "What should we do about the radio and window? I better go turn them off."

"Don't worry about it," Stratton said. "Maybe Sally will clean up when she's ready to leave. If not, I'll take care of it on our way out."

Chapter Eighteen

Pizza had never tasted so good. There, sitting across from the other four people in her little apartment, Denise finally felt complete and at peace. She was with her sister and her new friends. Whether or not Sally was real, it was evident that something pretty important had just happened.

The ghost's appearances and Aunt Flora's directives had brought life not only into the old theater, but also in her personal life, as well. Where she once was bitter and alone, she was now hopeful and surrounded by friends. Where she once felt unsure and depressed, she now felt confident and happy. Changes had taken place, both in her heart and in her life.

"Wow," Lindsay kept saying as Joanne filled her in on their little séance, or whatever it was.

Denise cast a quick glance in Ethan's direction. He'd been silent for the last hour, merely listening, sipping soda, and eating pepperoni pizza while the others hashed out what had happened downstairs.

His silence made her feel a little uncomfortable. Though she knew in her heart that she had felt an other-worldly presence, she was pretty sure all Ethan had felt was a cool breeze and more than a touch of humor, no matter what he said to the contrary.

The thought made her both embarrassed and sad; after all, how was she ever going to have a real relationship with someone who thought she was nuts? Deciding to see how he really did feel, she asked, "What did you think about tonight?"

"Interesting."

"That's it?"

"I've had worse evenings."

"Oh, come on, Ethan," Joanne chided. "Didn't you feel the slightest bit spooked when the window opened?"

"Maybe a little bit," he said after a pause.

"Real men don't admit fear," Stratton said through another bite of pizza. "Never."

Ethan grinned. "It's a sign of weakness."

Joanne picked up her paper plate, along with Stratton's and Lindsay's. "Well, you may be on a macho kick, but I felt more than a little creepy sitting in that theater. Are you *sure* you're going to be able to sleep here tonight, Denise?"

"I'm sure. Sally's never bothered me."

"I don't think she will, either," Lindsay said. "After all, you've cleared her name and are about to make her a star."

"Lindsay, don't you think you're being a little melodramatic?" Ethan asked.

Lindsay blinked twice. "No. Not at all. Denise has done something really cool." She cleared her throat. "Actually, the reason I came over was to tell you all about the latest meeting I've had with Mrs. Reece and the committee."

Joanne groaned softly. "I'm almost afraid to ask what happened."

"We now have sponsors and a date for the first performance. December 23rd! I'm going to start try-outs next week!"

Everyone clapped. Denise felt tears in her eyes. Lindsay's arrival was really a godsend, as was everything that had just happened. "That's great."

"That's great? It's unbelievable!" Joanne quipped. "Dee, how many times have we walked by this old place and wondered who was going to convince Aunt Flo to tear it down? I think it was on the chopping block at least two or three times in the last year. I recall Cameron saying that a few members of the city council had even written Flo to ask that she allow them to get rid of it."

"I'm so glad she always said no," Denise said.

"Ethan, you and Jeff and your team have worked wonders. It looks completely different."

"It should. I have plenty of sore muscles to show for it."

"He has been putting a lot of time on it," Lindsay said. "I've even been working in the hardware store so he could be here."

Joanne smiled. "This theater is going to be terrific. We'll have to have a party on opening night."

"You sound like Mom," Denise teased.

"No, Mom would have a gala, a parade, and a dress code. I was thinking more along the lines of pizza and cold drinks."

"That, I'd be up for," Stratton said.

After another hour, Lindsay left. Not long after that, Stratton and Joanne left as well. Then, only Ethan remained.

As Denise recalled how just an hour ago, she'd been wrapped up in his arms, she felt a little nervous. She wasn't sure if she was ready to rush back to him or keep their space. To calm herself, she wandered around her kitchen, cleaning off counters that were already clean.

"Tonight was really fun," she said inanely. "I mean, if you take out the part about being scared to death."

Motioning to her, he said, "Come sit down, Denise."

She sat. When he curved an arm around her, she leaned into him, loving the way his masculine frame made hers feel so feminine.

"Let's not talk about ghosts or theaters anymore," he said, rubbing her cheek with a callused thumb.

She turned to him. "What do you want to talk about?"

"Other, more interesting topics."

She pressed her head against his chest and closed her eyes when he brushed a hand through her hair. "Such as?"

"You."

"Me?"

"Well, and me too. Us. What are we going to do about us, Denise?"

She knew what she wanted to say, that she was completely over Chad and falling in love with him. But, she still wasn't sure if he felt the same way. Buying time, she said, "I'm not sure what you want me to say."

"Do you like me?"

She chuckled. "Isn't that something boys ask in sixth grade?"

"Maybe the boys you knew did; in sixth grade I was still only thinking about football, car magazines, and irritating my sisters. I guess I'm a slow learner."

There seemed to be nothing slow about Ethan Flynn at the moment. On the contrary, he seemed to be delivering a whole set of smooth moves.

"What were you doing in sixth grade?"

"Not looking at car magazines," she admitted. "Hmm. I think I was taking tap and cheerleading, and fighting with Joanne."

His fingers lazily caressed her shoulder. "No time for boys?"

"No. I really never had a serious boyfriend until I went to California. What about you? Did you have a girlfriend in high school?"

"I did, well for a month. Her name was Mary Jane Price and she had the most beautiful brown hair I'd ever seen."

Just to tease him, she whispered, "You have a thing for brunettes?"

"Not lately. Lately I can't stop thinking about a certain petite blonde."

She leaned closer. "I . . . I never thought I'd be ready for a relationship again."

"And now?"

"I have to admit that I've become very fond of a certain hardware store owner who has green eyes."

Those green eyes sparkled. "What are we going to do? Should we give in to our desires?" he teased.

His silly flirting made her smile. "And then what? What if things become serious?"

"What if they do? What if they already are?"

Denise knew they already were. And she distinctly remembered admitting that she had fallen for him. "I guess I'd be okay with that."

He glanced at her, eyes questioning. "You would, huh?"

"I would." She swallowed. "Actually, I have to admit

that I've entertained a thought in that direction once or twice."

"What else have your thoughts entertained? This?" he asked, leaning in and brushing her cheek with his lips. The innocent gesture brought back memories of the first time they had kissed and all the feelings that had come with their embrace as well, feelings that had not been completely without desire.

"Actually, I'm afraid I've entertained something more than that," she admitted.

He leaned closer and kissed the nape of her neck once. Twice. "Such as?"

His proximity made her bold, their frank conversation making her realize that they had nothing to lose. Either they were going to move forward, into a real relationship, or they were going to retreat back into mere friendship. Nothing in between. "A kiss again, like the one we shared the other day," she whispered, unable to tear her gaze away from his mouth, unable to stop her heart from beating double-time as those lips curved upward.

"So, you're thinking about one of those no-holds-barred kisses, where you don't think of another thing but how sweet it feels?"

He'd just about summed everything up. Her breath caught. "Pretty much."

"Good," he said, closing the gap between them once again. "Come here and kiss me."

She had no choice but to do what he asked.

Truthfully, there was nowhere else in the world she wanted to be and nothing else she would rather be doing.

As their lips met, and Ethan pulled her flush against his chest, Denise knew she'd been kidding herself. She wasn't just thinking about a relationship with him. She *was* in a relationship.

She wasn't worried about falling in love again. No matter what she said, or how hard she had fought it, she already had fallen in love again. Hard.

Chapter Nineteen

"Don't worry about a thing. I've got everything completely under control," Lindsay said when Denise strode down the stairs two weeks later.

Denise was pretty sure that instruction was about to be ignored. Complete chaos was reigning in the theater, and she already had a headache. It wasn't even eight in the morning.

Hammering had woken her up an hour ago, but it was the loud screech echoing through the bare walls that had made her decide to go downstairs to investigate. When she saw way too many people doing way too many things, Denise wondered why she had ever wanted to live on the top floor of the theater. She'd have to add it to her list of bad ideas.

"What is going on?" she asked, looking carefully at

Lindsay's stressed expression. "I thought I heard a scream a few minutes ago."

Amusement replaced worry in her friend's eyes. "Oh, that was number twenty-eight."

Denise realized she should have had more than one cup of coffee. "I don't quite follow you. Number twenty-eight?"

"We're casting for the Ghost of Christmas Past today. You know how scary he is." She leaned in closer. "Personally, I think a couple of our actors would do better with a little less enthusiasm."

Denise knew she would do better with a little less of everything.

The room was turned inside out. Costumes in piles. Paint cans in corners. Props on every flat surface.

Old rock tunes played on the boom box and just about every person in the place looked stressed enough to bolt. At least fifteen people, wearing makeshift costumes and numbers pinned to their chests, waited in line to try out for different parts in the play.

Ethan's friend Jeff had two of his buddies in the back storage room putting up shelves and painting trim.

And her mother was around with a whole host of women, dressed in heels and too much jewelry, sitting at card tables, planning who knew what.

Denise took a step back up the stairs. If her mother was here, that meant a crazy plan was not far behind. "When did my mother arrive?" she asked tentatively. Maybe they'd just gotten there. If that was the case,

Denise knew she'd have at least another hour before they were organized enough to summon her.

Lindsay rolled her eyes. "When does your mother ever leave? She was here when I got here at six." Lindsay popped out her left hip. "So . . . what have you been doing?"

Denise hopped up another step. "Sleeping."

"Hmmph."

"Hey, see the new backdrop? I worked on that until almost ten last night. And I attended a fundraising meeting with six of my mother's friends yesterday afternoon. I've been busy." When Lindsay still didn't look impressed, Denise added, "Plus, I told you I'd be around if you needed help."

Before the other woman could respond, a crash exploded from the storage room, and two of the kids auditioning for Tiny Tim looked liked they were about to get in a fist fight.

Denise knew it was time to either get involved in casting or bid a hasty retreat. "I think I'll go see Jeff," Denise said quickly before Lindsay could put her in charge of crowd control.

But Lindsay had already charged ahead and was shaking her finger at the long line of Tims. "Listen, you boys. Tiny Tim is sweet and good. And he's crippled. If you are roughhousing here, there's no place for you in the play."

"He started it," one of the boys retorted.

"I *am* crippled now," another said.

As Denise walked by, she couldn't help but chuckle. Although everything was crazy, it was a good crazy. Lively.

The theater was definitely seeing more life in it than she could ever remember. Aunt Flo would have been proud.

Peeking into the storage room, she said, "Jeff, is everything going okay in here?"

"It's great," he replied with a grimace. "The last shelf just fell on my foot. But now at least, I can try out for Tiny Tim."

Denise couldn't help it; she burst out laughing. "I'm sorry, it's just that those Tims are brawling over there."

Jeff laughed too. "Seriously, we're doing okay. We should be done in a half hour."

"Can I get you anything?"

"Nah."

She stood and talked with them for a few more minutes, scooting away cardboard costume boxes as she did so, and then knew she couldn't delay it any longer.

It was time to visit her mom.

"Hey," she said as she approached the two sets of card tables.

Daphne looked up from the drawing she was examining. "Hey, Dee. How are you?"

"Fine. What are you all doing?"

"We're planning the brochures at this table. They're working on the opening night gala."

"Gala?"

"Oh, yes. The mayor and city council decided we should commemorate opening night with a special celebration. All four Cincinnati news stations should be here.'

"We're offering free dessert," one lady said.

This was all news to her, and even though she was thankful for the help, it sounded as if things were getting even crazier. "Mom, I never okayed that. I was thinking more on the lines of pizza."

"I know, but I just happened to see the mayor at the mall yesterday. We got to talking, and one thing led to another. People are expecting more than pizza, dear. If you had been there, you would have agreed to the gala too."

Her mom was right. If Mayor Kincaid had asked her for a gala, she would have been nodding before he said another word. Moving on, she said, "So, what would you like me to do? I feel kind of bad with everyone working so hard while I was asleep. You should have called me."

"I figured you needed your sleep. After all, you were at Ethan's until after midnight, right?"

A couple of women tittered.

Denise felt her cheeks burn as the laughter grew. "How did you know that?"

"Oh, Missy or Cam or someone saw your car in his driveway."

Denise had a sneaking suspicion that not only had

her car been noticed, but Ethan's house had been monitored until she left.

"I wasn't there that late."

"A quarter to one might not seem late to you, but I know how grumpy you get without sleep. Besides, we had everything in hand."

"Ethan Flynn is so nice, Denise," Marianne McKinney said.

"Yes, ma'am."

"I've always liked him," another women added. "I like his style too. He's not pushy. I hate pushy salespeople."

"I do too."

"Rachel Penderton doesn't have a thing on you. No class."

"I called Walls and More. They're going to do my drapes for half the price," Mrs. McKinney announced. "I'm going to order a new set of chargers with the money I saved."

Denise didn't dare ask what chargers were. "So, how can I help?"

Her mother handed her a list. "Here you go. And, you're also on the list to judge. Maybe you could work on them in between the try-outs?"

"Sure. No problem."

Within minutes, Denise had a clipboard suspiciously like her mother's, a good half-inch of papers to read, and was sitting behind a desk, listening to try-outs for Scrooge, the ghosts, and everything in between.

.

For once, the noise level was at a minimum, everyone was on task, and nobody was having trouble.

She sighed in relief. It was going to work out. The theater was going to be great. Lindsay was going to ask to stay for the next fifty years. Her mother was going to help her plan, but not take over everything like a steamroller. And maybe even things between she and Ethan would progress. Maybe one day they'd get married, and she could taste what life was like for her siblings.

They'd settle into a routine; she could help him in his shop. Ethan could calm her down when everything seemed too overwhelming. They could spend cozy Sunday afternoons together.

The idea of spending quiet time with Ethan in the near future was tantalizing. Would they ever be able to steal away a moment or two together before the play?

At the moment, it didn't seem very likely.

"ACCKKK!"

This time, the scream sounded surprisingly real. Denise went running. As she entered the foyer, everyone was standing silently, gazing at the back window.

"What happened?" Denise asked, but she had the strange feeling that she already knew. Sally had decided to either join the party or put a stop to it.

"That window just popped open," one of her mother's friends said as she pointed to the window with a shaky finger. "Right there!"

"That's okay, it happens all the time," she said soothingly.

"You should get that fixed."

"I will."

"Wasn't Ethan Flynn in charge of the renovations?" someone asked, an edge to his voice. "Someone ought to talk to him. Denise, you don't want to get cheated on the repairs."

"I'm sure I won't."

"You better not."

"I tell you, if it is Ethan Flynn's fault, I'm going to think twice about retaining him for that basement we're refinishing," the same woman who'd just praised him moments ago complained. "If he can't handle something so elementary, I don't how he'd handle a whole room."

Denise couldn't bear to hear Ethan's name degraded, not after everything he'd done for her, and not after the super job he had done in a hundred-year-old theater. "It's the ghost," she said. "The window isn't Ethan's fault. The ghost likes to open it."

It hadn't seemed possible that the room could have gotten quieter. But it did.

But Denise didn't care. "Ethan's work has been terrific. I would recommend his work to anyone, anytime."

"But . . . a ghost?" Marianne McKinney said.

"It's Sally," Denise said, feeling more than a little self-conscious. "She's friendly, more or less. I'm beginning to think that her efforts are just to get attention."

"What do you do when that happens?"

"Nothing."

The questions kept coming. "Should we close the window or leave it open?" "Doesn't she talk to you or something?" "Are you frightened?" "What if the play gets sabotaged?"

Lindsay finally came to the rescue. "Everyone, I know you've all heard the rumors. Just because they're true doesn't mean that we need to change anything. If Sally is here right now, I'm hoping she'll give us tips for the ghosts in our play. Now, let's get back to work."

When everyone did as she bid, Denise heaved a sigh of relief.

Her mother came up to her and put an arm around her shoulders. "It's okay, you know," she said.

"What? The ghost?"

"No. Your feelings for Ethan."

The conversation was scaring her more than anything otherworldly. "Mom—"

"I've seen you two together. And I've seen the way you two look at each other. Mark my words. That's love."

Denise knew she felt that way, but that didn't mean she was ready for her mom to be involved. "It might be."

"I couldn't be more thrilled for you."

"Thank you."

Daphne turned dreamy. "I think a spring wedding would be a wonderful thing."

"Mom, keep your voice down! No one has said a

thing about weddings." Though, she had just been thinking about them, she realized.

"But they will. I think the two of you will make a great team. Ethan needs your help with the store, and you two can run this theater with Lindsay. Once you have children, you two will have a very full life."

Children? "Mom . . ."

"Oh, here he is. Hi, Ethan, we were just talking about you. Were your ears ringing?"

"Definitely," he said with a grin. "Is everything okay?"

"Great."

"Denise just defended you in front of all the ladies here. You ought to take her out."

Denise wondered if the conversation could get any more embarrassing.

"Don't worry about it."

Ethan blinked twice. "Where would you like to go?"

"I was thinking we could head into the city tonight. Get away. About seven o'clock?"

Like a girl in a trance, she nodded. "Seven would be just fine."

"Good. I'll see you then."

As soon as he walked over to his sister, Daphne hugged her hard. "I think this deserves a shopping trip. Don't you think?"

Denise could only nod.

Chapter Twenty

"It's rare to see *you* in a suit," Denise told Ethan when she opened the door.

"Suits aren't my style, but I don't mind putting on one every couple of months," he said smoothing a non-existent wrinkle from his jacket. "Even guys like me can get cleaned up."

She smiled at him, feeling suddenly shy. "Guys like you?"

"You know, hardware guys."

"I think you look very nice. Really handsome."

He held out a bouquet of flowers. "That's my line. I think you look terrific."

The flowers were an assortment of lilies, carnations, roses, and baby's breath. They were beautiful. "I love them! I'll just go put them in water."

He stood in the doorway, watching her. She felt more than a little self-conscious, wearing the new dress she and her mom had picked out at Kenwood Mall. It was more fitted than anything she usually wore and sported a slightly lower neck line. "I decided to dress up too."

"I can see why. It's pretty striking."

"It's new."

"I would have remembered if I'd seen it before."

She had nothing to say to that. In fact, she felt almost like a teenager, she was so tongue-tied. "It's really nice being alone with you," she finally blurted.

Ethan grinned. "I'm glad you think so."

"Oh! What I meant is that it seems like we've always had a bunch of other people around us, telling us what to do, where to go."

"I've never been fond of that, myself. I pretty much decided I didn't need another mom back in high school."

"I thought I was done with all that, but sometimes, it feels like I really need my mom," she admitted as they descended the stairs and walked out onto the street.

There, shiny and gleaming, was his Ford truck.

Ethan looked at her slim fitting dress. "Are you going to be able to get in this thing?"

"I hope so."

But it was easier said than done. Ethan had to help her climb into the cab, and by his grin, Denise had a feeling that he enjoyed a hefty sight of her thighs in the process.

"Did I tell you that I love that outfit?" he asked wickedly.

She bit her lip to hide her smile.

Dinner was wonderful. They talked about everything, from the country club to his sister and from high school sports to the latest sports statistics of the Bengals.

Ethan Flynn, for all of his good-old boy charm and down-to-earth ways, had insightful thoughts on just about everything.

They moved from their salads to their main courses with hardly a dull moment. And when they both declined dessert and coffee, Denise knew that there was much more between them than just eclectic conversations.

When his hand lingered on her hip as he helped her back into his truck, Denise knew that the last things she wanted to talk about were theaters, hardware stores, old relationships, or families.

The air was thick as he climbed into the cab beside her, filling the enclosed space with his heady cologne.

Without a word, he closed his door, then slid the keys into the ignition. Denise didn't know why, but she found herself watching every movement that he made. She was glancing at his hands again, remembering how solid they'd felt wrapped around her own and how tender his callused fingers had been when they'd brushed her hair away from her face the last time they'd kissed.

Instead of starting the ignition, Ethan just left the

keys dangling and with more finesse than she would have thought he possessed two months ago, pulled her into his arms and kissed her.

She kissed him right back.

All of a sudden, Ethan was kissing her like there was no tomorrow, right there in the Cork's parking lot. His muscles flexed as he pulled her close to him, and his hands curved around a hip. She gently positioned her jaw so he could deepen the kiss.

Denise held on for dear life. She reveled in his explorations, enjoyed his grunt of pleasure when she brushed her lips along his jaw, and willingly allowed him to take control and claim her mouth once again.

Her heart pounded, her pulse raced. She felt out of breath and heated and filled with every cliché she'd ever read.

And then, just as quickly, Ethan pulled away, breathing deeply, like he'd just run a race.

She sat there, her dress rumpled, riding high on her thighs, and stared at him once again as he ran his fingers through his hair.

Still, neither said a word.

He turned the ignition on, pulled the truck into first gear, and drove out of the parking lot. He pulled onto the freeway with enough speed to make her glad her seatbelt was on. As he merged with the light traffic, his fingers that had just been caressing her shoulders were now drumming the steering wheel.

"Denise," he said, finally breaking the silence.

"Yes?"

"I've been thinking."

She had too. She hoped he wanted to kiss her again, real soon. But, just to rile him up, she said, "About what?"

"You. Marriage."

Every emotion she was feeling rose to the surface. Surprise, desire, love, uncertainty. "Marriage?"

He switched lanes. "I love you," he said. "I love you very much."

She loved him too, but she hadn't told him and certainly hadn't expected to while driving sixty-five on the highway.

As if her silence was making him nervous, he started talking again. "You're the most beautiful thing I've ever seen in my life. From the first moment I saw you, I knew you were meant for me. I love your hair. I've dreamt about your hair," he added sheepishly. "And your lips. You've got great lips. And you kiss like a dream." He grunted. "I sound like a girl."

No, he sounded pretty good. She was just about to tell him so when he exited the freeway and started talking again.

"Now, we don't have to plan anything right away. I just wanted you to know I've been thinking about marriage."

She was just about to tell Ethan that she had also been thinking about love and marriage when he began again.

"Don't tell me that we don't match, because I think

we do. I like the fact that you're quiet. The last thing I want is to be with a non-stop talker the rest of my life. My sister talks more than any person on the planet. Frankly, talking is overrated."

He pulled onto a side street. She noticed that it was his street, not hers. "I like the fact that you worry about things and other people, both dead and alive." He parked in the driveway. "I think we'd be great together. You've got to give us a chance. You really need to think about it."

But before she could even open her mouth to say 'yes,' Ethan Flynn unbuckled his seat belt, unbuckled hers, and kissed her again as if he was dying of thirst and she was his last glass of water.

He consumed her. He wasn't letting her go, wasn't giving her a chance to deny him. And she was in no hurry to do anything.

Finally, when she was so limp she felt like a rag doll, he lifted his head. "Denise?" he asked.

She drew a fortifying breath. "Are you going to let me speak now?"

Silently, he nodded.

Quickly, Denise thought of everything she wanted to say, about how he'd given her a new reason to wake up in the morning, about how she admired him, about how she thought he was particularly handsome and how his kisses had set fire to her heart and the rest of her body.

But all she had the energy for was, "I love you too."

His eyes widened. "Yeah?"

She nodded.

"And, I think marriage would be great . . . one day."

He smiled slowly. "When were you thinking?"

"Six months? A year?"

"That sounds good," he murmured as their lips met again. When they parted, a shudder passed through him, and the look he gave her was one of triumph. "You want to come in for a little while? I promise I won't let things go too far . . . but I don't want to say goodnight yet."

She didn't either.

"Invite me in, Ethan," she said, far more clearly than she thought she could. "I don't want to say goodnight, either."

"Thank God," he said, then got out on his side, helped her out, and walked her into his place.

Comet greeted them at the door. Ethan petted him, then drew her to the couch. "I'm not going to let you change your mind, Denise. I love you too much."

"Have I ever told you that I think Denise Flynn sounds much better than Denise Reece?"

"I agree," he murmured. "I think Denise Flynn sounds downright perfect." He waited two beats as he smoothed back her hair. "Just like you."

Denise knew there was nothing to say to that.

And no reason to try.

Chapter Twenty-one

"Opening night is in five days," Lindsay proclaimed.

Denise couldn't forget. The whole theater was nutty almost twenty-four hours a day. Lindsay was in her element, and so was her mom and her gang of committee members, but Denise was feeling more than ready to take a break, which was why she'd asked her parents if she could move back in with them for eight months until she and Ethan were married.

Everyone soon realized that it would make the most sense for Lindsay to live on the top floor of the theater, and Lindsay seemed happy to be there.

So far, she hadn't seen or heard much from the ghost, though Denise had smelled the talcum powder more than once. She'd kept Sally in mind when she'd written a summary about the history of the theater,

Aunt Flo's donation, and finally her decision to start it up again.

She'd even made the connection with the theater's haunted past to Sally's ruined reputation. So far, she'd heard nothing but encouraging words about it since the article had been printed in the *Payton Registrar*.

But, Denise still felt compelled to ask Lindsay about Sally.

"Have you had any experiences with the ghost?"

Lindsay paled a little bit. "Maybe."

"What does that mean?"

"It means maybe I'm not laughing as much when someone mentions her."

"What happened? Are you scared?"

"No." Lindsay leaned forward. "Listen, don't mention a word of this to anybody, but I talked to her the other night."

"What? You heard her?"

"No. But she was playing that blasted boom box again, this time at one in the morning. I asked her if she could be more respectful to me. I mean, I am a working woman. She ought to be able to understand that."

Denise hid a smile. "What happened?"

"Well, I simply said that if she was going to listen to music, either she should move the boom box to the basement, or pick better times."

"Do you have any idea what she wants to do?"

"Kind of. The music went right off. I think we reached an agreement." Lindsay coughed. "I, um . . . I read her your article, about how you found out that Ronald was really just a jerk. I think that made her happy."

"Wow."

"But don't tell anyone I said this. I'll talk about ghosts and such when we're directing plays, but I don't want anyone thinking that I'm obsessed or anything."

"I won't."

"So, how are things with my brother?"

Denise glanced at Lindsay, wondering what had brought on that whole other subject. Was she just really tired of thinking about the ghost or worried about her brother? "Fine."

"He acts like the sun rises and sets on you. I heard him talking about you to our parents the other day."

Feeling relief, Denise smiled. "I've talked to them on the phone. They seem really nice."

"They are. You're going to love them. They're going to love you too." As she glanced at her more carefully, she scowled. "You're so . . . feminine."

Denise didn't know what had brought that on. "Is that bad?"

"No! Ethan loves it."

"Then why did you just frown at me?" she asked, chiding.

"I'm sorry, I didn't mean to. I just know that when my parents come in town and see the two of us side by side, it's just going to remind everyone that I'm more like Ethan than you."

"You should be, you're his sister."

"I know, but I also know there's a part of my mother who always wished for the daughter who loved dolls and tea parties, not climbing trees and baseball."

"Just for your information, I've seen you act very girly."

"That was acting! I think that's why I became an actress, so I could be everything to everybody."

"I learned the hard way that not being true to yourself can lead to trouble. When I was in California, I never did completely fit in, because I never was being completely myself."

"Ethan likes you for who you are."

She thought about Ethan, about his smile, and how he could repair anything. He was still so dedicated to his classes, even though there was so much else going on in his life. She loved his steadfastness and thoughtfulness.

"I like Ethan for who he is too."

"Did I just hear my name?" Ethan asked, as he walked in the main room. "What are you two talking about?"

As Lindsay's eyes became big, Denise motioned that their conversation would stay private. "Oh, we were just talking about how there's someone for everyone."

He leaned close and kissed her on her forehead. "Is that right?"

"Yep. You are perfect for me."

"I feel the same way."

"Oh, for heaven's sakes," Lindsay said with a scowl. "Enough of the lovey-dovey stuff."

"I'll do my best to keep it at a minimum," Ethan said, his eyes glinting. "Actually, I wondered what you needed help with."

"Take your pick," Lindsay said with a wave of her hand. "Join a committee or do crowd control."

A crash startled the three of them. "What's that? Do you think it was the ghost?" Denise asked.

"I think more likely it was the props person. He won't listen to any of my suggestions about organizing. I've got to go."

And off she went, leaving Denise and Ethan alone in a temporarily lonely room.

"This place is out of control," he said, his voice wry.

She chuckled. "I know. I don't know where to turn first."

"That's easy," he murmured, pulling her into his arms. "Turn right here."

Looping her hands around his neck, she murmured, "Is this okay?"

"Perfect."

"I'm glad," she said. In his arms was where she wanted to be.

Epilogue

The curtain closed. Lights came on. After a second's silence, the crowd burst to their feet, cheering "Bravo" and "Encore!"

As the curtain rose slowly and the cast of *Scrooge* began to take their bows, Denise felt an intense feeling of satisfaction. They'd done it.

They'd remodeled, refurbished, and redecorated the old theater.

They'd somehow managed to produce, direct, and perform a play there too.

They hadn't let money, groups of committee members, ghosts, or ex-girlfriends get in the way.

And it had been a rousing success.

Aunt Flo would have been pleased. Denise knew it in

her heart. Finally, after years of neglect, the old place, now named the Sally McGraw Theater, was standing tall and proud.

And she'd had a part in it.

"I loved the play," her mom said, hugging her tight. "I can't believe you pulled it off."

"*We* pulled it off. You, Ethan, Lindsay . . . it took everyone to make it a success," Denise pointed out.

"Maybe. But we had you guiding us, cheering us on. You should be proud of yourself."

"I am," she admitted. "I thought we did a great job."

More of her family joined them. One by one, each kissed her cheek, hugged her hard, or clasped her hand. Everyone was there—her dad, whose eyes twinkled with fatherly pride, Mary Beth, Cameron, Maggie, Joanne and Stratton, Kevin and Missy and their little girl Tam, and Jeremy, Missy, and Bryan.

"Guess what?" Joanne asked, her expression filled with delight.

"You've got another building to save?" someone asked.

"No. I'm pregnant! Finally!" she exclaimed.

Denise caught her sister's eye. Something passed between them. Something special between sisters. It had to do with late nights when they were nine, shared clothes, and doing each other's hair.

"Congratulations," Denise said softly.

Joanne swallowed hard. "Thanks."

Hugs were given again.

Finally the lights came on completely, and people began to file out on both sides.

"I guess we ought to move," Jim Reece said. "We seem to be in the middle of everything."

"You all ready to go to the gala?" Daphne asked. "It's going to be wonderful!" Hugging Joanne, she exclaimed, "And now we even have more to celebrate."

Denise couldn't help but feel the same way. "I'll be right there. As soon as I find Ethan."

"There he is," her dad said, pointing toward the stage. As Denise turned, she saw him giving Lindsay a hug. Next to them stood their parents. When Ethan caught her eye, he smiled brightly.

"I do like that Ethan Flynn," Daphne said to everyone as they all parted to make their ways to the parking lot. "He's so handy."

"He is that," Joanne said with enough humor to make them all laugh.

And as Denise waited for Ethan to make his way to her, she knew that everything was wonderful. She'd found love right there at home. She'd found Ethan . . . and her family.

Just as she was about to become a Flynn, she remembered how special it was being a Reece.